E-Z DICKENS SUPERHERO BOOK 1:

TATTOO ANGEL: THE THREE

Cathy McGough

Stratford Living Publishing

WHAT READERS ARE SAYING...

FIVE STARS - READERS' FAVORITE   BOOK ONE TATTOO ANGEL

"After a tragedy leaves a boy an orphan, he discovers he has special powers that will help him save lives in the young adult adventure book E-Z Dickens Superhero (Book One: Tattoo Angel) by Cathy McGough. Thirteen-year-old Ezekiel Dickens, E-Z to his friends and family, is an average boy with a passion for baseball. An accident deprives him of his parents and condemns him to a wheelchair,

Riddles and ghosts abound in the young adult supernatural adventure, E-Z Dickens Superhero by Cathy McGough. With a positive message, this story can help those suffering from trauma and injury to heal and change their perspective."

FOUR STARS - AMAZON REVIEWER - BOOK ONE: TATTOO ANGEL

When E-Z wakes up in the hospital after a tragic accident, his parents are dead and the 13-year-old can't move his toes. Although confined to a wheelchair, he discovers he can fly - with wings growing from his arms where tattoos should be. He's not left to fend for himself in a strange new world, as he has his Uncle Sam who steps in to raise him, along with supernatural entities that appear when you least expect it.

I like E-Z. He's quirky, and even though an accident derailed his dreams of becoming a professional baseball player, he doesn't feel sorry for himself and pulls the reader along with him. His attitude is uplifting (despite the fact that he has wings, no pun intended). Readers will cheer for him. It's good to see a disabled character playing a central role in the plot, rather than staying on the sidelines, contributing little to the action. Applause for the author. I also like the concept of ghosts giving E-Z special powers, but I wish they had become more developed as other main characters. Nevertheless, a clever story. The book will appeal to young teens. Well done.

FIVE STARS - Amazon Reviewer - BOOK TWO: THE THREE

E-Z DICKENS SUPER HERO BOOK TWO: THE THREE by Cathy McGough is a great superhero adventure story. The main characters, E-Z, Lia and Alfred, will take you on an adventure with surprises you don't expect. And what do the Archangels have to do with their mission? Find out for yourself. I really enjoyed the plot, the writing style and the story, which kept me in suspense until the last chapter.

I recommend this book to anyone who likes superheroes, suspense, action, adventure, teenagers, YA or fiction.

Contents

Dedication

For Dorothy who believed.

BOOK ONE:
TATTOO ANGEL

PROLOGUE

T HE FIRST CREATURE FLEW onto E-Z's chest and landed, with his chin thrust forward and hands on his hips. He turned once, clockwise. Spinning faster, from the flutter of his wings a song emanated. The song was a low moan. A sad song from the past in celebration of a life that was no more. The creature leaned back, head resting against E-Z's chest. The spinning stopped but the song continued playing.

The second creature joined in, doing the same ritual, while turning anti-clockwise. They created a new song, minus the beep-beeps and zoom-zooms. For when they sang, onomatopoeia was not required. Whereas in everyday conversation with humans it was. This song overlaid the other and became a joyful, high-pitched celebration. An ode for things to come, of a life yet unlived. A song for the future.

A spray of diamond dust burst from their golden eye sockets as they turned in perfect synchronicity. The diamond dust sprayed from their eyes onto E-Z's sleeping body. The exchange continued, until it covered him with diamond dust from head to toe.

The teenager continued sleeping soundly. Until the diamond dust pierced his flesh – then he opened his mouth to scream but no sound emanated.

"He's waking up, beep-beep."

"Lift him, zoom-zoom."

Together they raised him up as he opened his glazed-over eyes.

"Sleep more, beep-beep."

"Feel no pain, zoom-zoom."

Cradling his body, the two creatures accepted his pain into themselves.

"Rise up, beep-beep," he commanded.

And the wheelchair, raised up. And, positioning itself under E-Z's body, it waited. When a droplet of blood descended, the chair caught it. Absorbed it. Consumed it – like it was a living thing.

As the chair's power increased, it also gained strength. Soon the chair could hold its master in mid-air. This allowed the two creatures to complete their task. Their task of joining the chair and the human. Binding them, for all eternity with the power of diamond dust, blood, and pain.

As the teenager's body shook, the punctures on his skin healed. The task was complete. The diamond dust was a part of his essence. Thus, the music came to a stop.

"It is done. Now he is bullet-proofed. And he has super strength, beep-beep."

"Yes, and it is good, zoom-zoom."

The wheelchair returned to the floor, and the teenager onto his bed.

"He will have no memory of it, but his real wings will begin functioning very soon beep-beep."

"What about the other side effects? When will they begin, and will they be noticeable zoom-zoom?"

"That I do not know. He may have physical changes...it's a risk worth taking to reduce the pain, beep-beep."

"Agreed zoom-zoom."

CAUSE

ALL FAMILIES HAVE DISAGREEMENTS. Some argue about every little thing. The Dickens family agreed on most things. Music wasn't one of them.

"Come on Dad," twelve-year-old E-Z said. "I'm bored and they're playing an all-Muse weekend on the satellite right now."

"Didn't you bring your headphones?" his mother Laurel asked.

"They're in my backpack in the trunk." He sighed.

"We could always stop and get them..."

Martin, the boy's father who was driving checked the time. "I'd like to get to the cabin in the mountains before it gets dark. Muse is fine with me. Besides, we'll be there soon."

Laurel turned the dial on the satellite system in their brand-new red convertible. She hesitated for a moment on Classic Rock. The announcer said, "Next up is the Kiss anthem I Wanna Rock N Roll All Night. Don't touch that dial."

"Wait, that's a good song!" the boy shouted.

"What, no more Muse?" Laurel asked, keeping her hand on the dial.

"After Kiss, okay?"

"*Kiss* it is then," Martin said, as he flipped on the windshield wipers. It wasn't raining yet, but thunder was booming. Twigs and other debris were whipping in and out of their vehicle as they made their way up the mountain.

Laurel sneezed and put a bookmark onto her page. She crossed her arms shivering. "That wind is sure howling. Mind if we put the top up?"

"I vote yes," E-Z said, removing twigs from his blond hair.

THWACK.

There was no time to scream—when the music died.

The boy's ears were still ringing from the sound coupled with the explosion of four airbags. Blood dripped down his forehead as he touched the thing on his legs: a tree. Blood pooled in and around the wooden intruder. He ran his finger along the trunk of the tree. It felt like skin; he was the tree, and the tree was him.

"Mom? Dad?" he sobbed, chest heaving. "Mom? Dad? Please answer!"

He needed to call for help. Where was his phone? The impact of the crash had thrown it clear. He could see it, but it was too far to reach. Or was it? He was a catcher, and some said his throwing arm was like rubber. He concentrated, stretched and stretched until he got it.

The signal was strong as his bloodied fingers pushed 9-1-1, then disconnected. For them to find him, he needed to use the new enhanced service. He typed E9-1-1. This gave the the authorities permission to access his location, phone number and address.

"Emergency Services. What is your emergency?"

"Help! We need help! Please. My parents!"

"First tell me, how old are you? What's your name?"

"I'm twelve. They call me E-Z."

"Please verify your address and phone number."

He did.

"Hi E-Z. Tell me about your parents. Can you see them? Are they conscious?"

"I, I can't see them. A tree fell on the car, on them and my legs. Help. Please."

"We're getting your location now."

E-Z closed his eyes.

"E-Z?" Louder, "E-Z!"

The boy came to. "I, sorry, I."

"We're sending a helicopter. Try to stay awake. Help is on the way."

"Thank you," his eyes drooped closed, he forced them open. "I must stay awake. She said to stay awake." All he wanted to do was sleep, sleep to end all the pain.

Above him, two lights, one green and one yellow flickered in front of his eyes. For a second, he thought he saw tiny wings flapping as the two objects hovered.

"He's in a bad way," the green one said, moving in to take a closer look.

"Let's help him," the yellow one said hovering higher.

E-Z raised his hand, to swat the flickering lights. A high-pitched sound hurt his ears.

"Do you agree to help us?" the lights sang.

"I do. Help me."

Then everything went black.

EFFECT

S AM, E-Z's UNCLE WAS in the hospital when he woke up. The boy didn't ask the question – where his parents were – because he didn't want to hear the answer. If he didn't know, he could pretend they were fine. That they'd walk into his room and throw their arms around him any minute now. But in the back of his mind he knew, in fact he believed that they were dead. He imagined it in his mind, how he'd throw back the covers and run to them and they'd come together in a group hug and cry about how lucky they were. But wait a minute, why couldn't he wiggle his toes? He tried again, concentrating hard but nothing happened.

Sam who was watching said, "There's no uncomplicated way to tell you this," all the while he was fighting back a sob.

"My legs," E-Z said, "I, I can't feel them."

Uncle Sam squeezed his nephew's hand. "Your legs…"

"Oh no. Don't tell me. Just don't."

He wrenched his hand free from his uncle. He covered his face, creating a barrier between himself and the world as tears rolled down his cheeks.

Uncle Sam hesitated. His nephew was already in tears, already grieving and yet he had to tell him about his parents. There was no easy way to say it, so he blurted it out, "Your parents. My brother and your mom...they didn't make it."

Knowing and hearing the words were two different things. One made it a fact. E-Z threw his head back and howled like a wounded animal, shaking, and wanting to run away, anywhere. Just away.

"E-Z, I'm here for you."

"No! It's not true. You're lying. Why are you lying to me?" He thrashed about, balling up his fists and pounding them down into the mattress as he raged and raged with no sign of stopping.

Sam pushed the button near the bed. He tried to calm him, but E-Z was out of control, thrashing and swearing. Two nurses arrived; one inserted the needle while the other with Sam tried to keep him still and he whispered softly that everything was going to be okay.

Sam looked on, as his nephew in dreamland or wherever he was now – mustered up a smile. He cherished that smile, thinking it would be a while before he saw one again on his nephew's face. It was going to be a long and difficult road ahead. His nephew would have to face the day when his life fell apart head on. Once he did that, he could fight and together they could build him a brand-new life. New – different – not the same. Nothing would ever be the same again.

All because they were in the wrong place at the wrong time. Victims of nature: a tree. A tree which became nature's weapon through human neglect. The wooden structure had been dead, roots above the ground vying for attention for years. And when they told him it had been marked with an X for cutting down in the spring – he wanted to scream.

Instead, he called the best lawyer he knew. He wanted someone to pay – to pick up the bill for two lives cut short too soon, and for his nephew's shattered legs and life.

But what was the point? Nothing could change the past – but in the future he would help his nephew find his way. At that moment Sam formulated a plan.

Sam resembled a grown-up version of Harry Potter (minus the scar.) As E-Z's only living relative, he'd take on his nephew's care. A role he'd neglected in the past. He'd try to be like his older brother Martin – not to replace him.

He shook off the excuses, bubbling up inside. Trying to get him to use work to relieve him from responsibility. He would walk away, blot out all obligations. Then he could stop recriminating himself. Hating himself for all the lost time.

While his nephew slept on, he called the CEO of his Software Company. As an accomplished Senior Programmer in the top of his field – he hoped they would come to a compromise. He told them what he wanted to do.

"Sure, Sam. You can work remotely. Nothing will change. You do what you must do. We're with you. Family first – always."

When he disconnected, he returned to his nephew's bedside. For now, he would move into the family home, so E-Z could remain near his friends and school. Together they would put the pieces back together again and rebuild his life. That's if he didn't totally freak out. As a bachelor, he had little to no experience with kids – let alone teenagers.

✳✳✳

AFTER LEAVING THE HOSPITAL – compelled by fate – they had no choice but to create a bond that went beyond blood.

E-Z resisted, in denial thinking he could do it all himself. In the end he had no choice but to accept the help on offer.

Sam stepped up – was there for him – like he knew what his nephew needed before he asked.

And he was there for E-Z on the second worst day of his life – when he was told he'd never walk again.

"Come on in," Dr. Hammersmith, one of the top Orthopedic Neurologist Surgeons said.

In his wheelchair, E-Z entered, followed by Sam.

Hammersmith was famous for fixing the unfixable and he was going to fix him. In previous consultations he'd promised the youngster he would play baseball again.

"I'm sorry," Hammersmith said. After a few seconds of uncomfortable silence, he filled it by shuffling some papers.

"What is it exactly that you are sorry about?" E-Z inquired, pushing with all his might to move forward in his seat. Unable to accomplish the task, he remained where he was.

"What he asked," Sam said, moving effortlessly forward in his seat.

Hammersmith cleared his throat. "We hoped since everything was functioning normally the paralysis might be temporary. That's why I sent you for more tests and suggested some physical therapy. There is no doubt now, I'm sorry to tell you E-Z, but you'll never walk again."

"How can you do this to him?" Sam asked.

The finality of his words sunk in. "Get me out of here, Uncle Sam!"

"Wait," Hammersmith said, unable to look them in the eyes. "I asked for help, from colleagues around the world. Their conclusion was the same."

"Thanks a bunch."

"E-Z, it's time for you to move on. I don't want to give you more false hope. "

Sam stood, putting his hands on the wheelchair handles.

"We'll get a second opinion and a third and a fourth!"

"You can do that," Hammersmith said, "but we already did. If there was anything new, out there - anything we could tap into - then we would do it. Things may change in your lifetime E-Z. The field of stem cell research is making advances. In the meantime, I don't want you living your life for the ifs and the maybes."

Then directed at Sam,

"Don't let your nephew waste his life. Help him to rebuild and get back to the land of the living. Oh, and I hate to bring this up, but we'll need the wheelchair back soon – seems we have a bit of a shortage. If you wouldn't mind making other arrangements."

"Fine," Sam said, as they left Hammersmith's office without speaking. He put the wheelchair into the trunk, fastened their seatbelts and started up the car.

"It'll be okay."

E-Z who had tears rolling down his cheeks, wiped them away. "I'm sorry."

"You never have to apologize to me kiddo, for showing your feelings."

Sam slammed his fists down on the steering wheel, then pulled out of the parking spot squealing his tires.

They drove along without speaking for a few moments, then he reached over and turned on the radio. It gulfed the silence between the two and gave E-Z the opportunity to cry it out without feeling self conscious.

By the time they turned into the driveway at home, they were calm and hungry. The plan was to binge watch a few programs and order in pizza.

A few days later a brand-new wheelchair arrived.

✳✳✳

TWO LIGHTS: ONE YELLOW and one green flickered near E-Z's new wheelchair.

"This one won't do, beep-beep."

"I agree, it won't do at all. He needs something lighter, stronger, fireproof, bulletproof, and absorbent, zoom-zoom."

"You-know-who said we shouldn't waste any time – so, let's do it, before the human wakes up, beep-beep."

The lights danced around the wheelchair. One replaced the metal and the other the tires. When they completed the process, the chair looked the same as it did before, but it wasn't.

E-Z whispered in his sleep.

"Let's get out of here! Beep beep!"

"Right behind you! Zoom zoom!"

And so, they did while the youngster slept on.

✳✳✳

A YEAR LATER AND it seemed now to E-Z, that Uncle Sam had always been there. Not that he'd replaced his parents. No, he'd never be able to do that, in fact he wouldn't try – but they got on. They were mates. They were more than that, they were family. The only family the thirteen-year-old had left in the world.

"I want to thank you," he said, trying not to get teary-eyed.

"You don't have to thank me, kiddo."

"But I do, Uncle Sam, without you, I would have thrown in the towel."

"You're made of stronger stuff than that."

"I'm not. Since the accident I get scared, I mean really scared. I've been having nightmares."

"We all get scared; it helps if you talk about it. I mean if you want to talk to me about it."

"It happens sometimes at night – when you're asleep. I don't want to wake you."

"I'm next door and the walls aren't that thick. Just shout for me and I'll be there. I don't mind."

"Thanks, I hope I won't need to but it's good to know."

They went back to watching television and never discussed the matter again.

Until one night, when E-Z woke up screaming and Sam as promised was there.

He turned on the light. "I'm here. Are you all right?"

E-Z was clinging to the edge of the bed, like someone who was about to go over a cliff. He helped him back onto the mattress.

"Better now?"

"Yes, thanks."

"Feel like talking about it? I can make some cocoa."

"With marshmallows?"

"Goes without saying. Be right back."

"Okay." E-Z closed his eyes for a second, and the high-pitched noises resumed. He covered his ears and watched the yellow and green lights as they danced before his eyes. He removed his hands, hearing his Uncle's bare feet as they slapped along the corridor.

"Here you go," Sam said, placing a mug of hot cocoa into his nephew's hand. He parked himself in the wheelchair where he sipped and sighed.

With his left hand, E-Z swatted the air, nearly spilling his drink.

"What are you doing?"

"Can't you hear it? That ear-splitting sound?"

Sam listened intently, nothing. He shook his head. "If you're hearing something strange, why are you trying to swat it away?"

E-Z focused on his hot drink, then swallowed a mini-marshmallow. "I guess you can't see the lights then?"

"Lights? What kind of lights?"

"Two lights: one green and one yellow. About the size of the end of your finger. Here on and off – since the accident. Piercing my ears and blinking in front of my eyes. Annoying me."

Sam went to the headboard and looked on from his nephew's perspective. He didn't expect to see anything – and of course he didn't – the effort was for reassurance. "Nope, but tell me more, so I can better understand how it started."

"At the accident, I saw two lights, yellow and green and, don't laugh, but I think they spoke to me. That's why I've been having nightmares."

"What kind of lights? You mean, like Christmas lights?"

"Uh, no not like Christmas lights. It's nothing. They're gone now. Probably Post-traumatic stress disorder, or a flashback."

"PTSD or a flashback are two vastly different things. I wonder if, you should talk to someone. I mean someone, besides me."

"You mean like my friends?"

"No, I mean a professional."

POP.

POP.

They were back again. Blinking in front of his nose and making him cross-eyed. He held back. Tried not to swat them away. As Sam took his cup with one hand and felt his forehead with the other, he slapped the air. "Get away from me!"

Sam looked on as his nephew froze, like an ice sculpture at the Winter Festival. Sam snapped his fingers in front of his eyes, but there was no reaction. E-Z sighed and leaned back, took a deep breath and within seconds, was snoring like a trooper. Sam pulled the covers up. He kissed his nephew on the forehead, then returned to his room. Eventually he dropped off to sleep.

The next day, Sam suggested E-Z write down his feelings, perhaps in a diary. Meanwhile he'd inquire about booking an appointment with a professional.

"You mean a shrink?"

"Or a psychologist. And in the meantime, write it down. When you see them, what they look like – record the sightings."

"A diary, I mean, who do I look like, Oprah Winfrey?"

"No," Sam said. "Kiddo, you're having nightmares, hearing high-pitched noises, and seeing lights. They may be a sign of, like you said PTSD or something medical. I need to investigate and speak to your doctor, get his advice. Meanwhile, writing down your thoughts, keeping a journal might help. Plenty of men have written diaries or kept a journal."

"Name one whose name I'd recognize?"

"Let's see, Leonardo da Vinci, Marco Polo, Charles Darwin."

"I mean someone from this century."

"You already mentioned Oprah."

✱✱✱

E-Z'S MENTAL HEALTH IMPROVED after a few sessions with a therapist/counsellor. She was nice and didn't judge the teenager, like he was afraid she would. Instead, she offered suggestions and specific strategies to calm and help him. She, like his Uncle Sam had also suggested he write it all down – in a journal or diary.

Instead, he authored a short story for a school assignment inspired by his mother's favourite bird: a dove. After he received an A+ on his paper, his teacher entered his story into a province-wide writing contest. At first, he was upset she'd entered his story without asking him. But when he won, he was incredibly happy. Since then, his teacher entered his story into a country-wide competition.

While his nephew was delving into the art of writing, Sam was taking on a new hobby: genealogy. One night when they were having dinner, he blurted:

"Now that you've written a short story and had some success, maybe you should try to write a novel."

"Me? A novel? No way."

"You have writer's blood," Uncle Sam revealed. "Through tracing our history, I've discovered you and I are related to the one and only Charles Dickens."

"Maybe YOU should write a novel, then." He laughed.

"I'm not the one with an award-winning short story."

The green and yellow lights flickered above his plate. At least he couldn't hear that high-pitched noise with Uncle Sam droning on.

".... After all, you, and I, we are cousins across time with Charles Dickens. Look at everything you've overcome. You're an amazing kid - what have you got to lose?"

His name is Ezekiel Dickens, and this is his story.

CHAPTER 1

IN THE FIRST THIRTEEN years of his life, he was known by several names. Ezekiel, his birthname. E-Z, his nickname. Catcher on his baseball team. Short story writer. Son to his parents. Nephew to his uncle. Best friend. Now they had a new name for him.

Not that he minded the "c" word. In fact, some of the alternatives he preferred less. Like the comments some people said, because they thought they were politically correct. "Oh, there's the kid who's confined to a wheelchair." They said this while pointing at him – like they thought he was hearing impaired, too. Or they'd say, "I was sorry to hear that you're a wheelchair user, now." That made him cringe. But the one that sent him over the edge, was "Oh, you're the kid who uses a wheelchair now." Seeing anyone, especially a younger person in a wheelchair made some people feel uncomfortable. If they felt that way, why did they *have to* say something?

This sparked a memory from long ago. A memory of his parents, watching the movie Bambi on television on a rainy Saturday afternoon. Mom made her famous popcorn balls. They had soda, M&Ms, marshmallows, and dad's favourite Twizzlers. Thumper the rabbit said, "If you can't say something nice, don't say nothing at all." When Bambi's mother died, it was the first time he'd ever seen his mother and father cry over a movie. Because he was so shocked at their behaviour, he, himself didn't shed a tear.

Some of the yahoos at school, were calling him "tree boy." A few were fellow athletes who once looked up to him when he was king behind the plate. He hated the tree boy reference. He didn't feel sorry for himself (not most of the time) and he didn't want anyone to feel sorry for him either.

When the time came for him to return to school on that very first day, he did it with the help of his friends. PJ (short for Paul Jones) and Arden supported and pushed him, as needed. They were soon known as The Tornado Trio. Mostly because wherever they went chaos ensued. That's when E-Z learned to expect the unexpected.

So, when his friends popped round one morning to pick him up for school a few months later – then said they weren't going – he wasn't too surprised. When they said they had to blindfold him – that wasn't expected.

In the backseat he asked. "Where are we going?" No reply. "Am I going to like it?"

"Yes," his friends said.

"Then why the cloak and dagger?"

"Because it's a surprise," PJ said.

"And you'll appreciate it more, once we're there."

"Well, I can't run away." He scoffed.

Arden's mother parked. "Thanks Mom," he said.

"Call me when you need me to collect you," she said.

The two friends helped E-Z into his wheelchair and off they went.

"Is it just me, or does this chair seem lighter every time we take it out?" Arden asked.

"It's you!" PJ replied.

As they made their way across unlevel ground, E-Z could smell freshly cut grass. When his friends pulled off the blindfold – he was at the baseball field. Tears welled up in his eyes when he saw his former teammates, the opposing team, and Coach Ludlow. They were in full uniform, lined up along the freshly chalked baseline.

"Welcome back!" they cheered.

E-Z brushed the tears away with his sleeve as the chair moved nearer to the playing field. Since the accident had taken away his dream to play professional baseball, he'd avoided the game. With a lump in his throat, he was so filled with emotion he couldn't catch his breath.

"He's lost for words," PJ said, giving Arden a nudge with his elbow.

"That's a first."

"Thanks, guys. You weren't wrong about this being a surprise."

"Wait here," his friends instructed.

E-Z was left alone to take in the view of the baseball diamond. The place that had once been his favourite place on earth. He teared up again, watching the green grass shimmer in the sunlight. He wiped them away when his friends returned carrying a bag of equipment.

Arden leaned in, "Surprise mate, you're catching today!"

"What do you mean? I can't play in this!" he said, thumping his hands on the wheelchair arms.

"Here, watch this, while we get you fitted up," PJ said, as he handed over his phone and pushed play.

E-Z watched in amazement as players like him, made their way onto the baseball field. He looked more closely at their chairs which had modded wheels. A player rolled up to the plate, connected with the ball, and zoomed around the bases.

"Wow! This is awesome!"

"If they can do it, so can you!" Arden said as he put the knee pads onto his friend's legs while PJ secured the chest protector. On the way out onto the field, his friends tossed him the catcher's mask and his glove.

"Batter up!" Coach Ludlow called.

The pitcher tossed the first fastball right in the zone and he caught it.

The second pitch was a pop up. E-Z went for it, zooming over, lifting himself up. Reaching. He even surprised himself when he caught it. They hadn't noticed, but he'd raised himself up. His butt had left the seat of his chair, and he had no idea how he'd done it.

"Wow," PJ said, "that was an excellent catch."

"Yeah, you probably would have missed it, if it hadn't been for the chair."

E-Z smiled and continued playing. When the game was over, he felt good. Normal. He thanked the guys for getting him back into the swing of things.

"Next time, you hit," PJ said.

E-Z scoffed as Arden's Mom took them through the drive through, then back to school. If they hurried, they would make it in time before their next class started. Students jammed the halls, as he rolled along to his locker. His classmates heard the slap-slapping sound of the tires on the linoleum floor – and they parted the way.

E-Z had been the first kid to require wheelchair access at his school, but he was already a legend before he lost the use of his legs. It had taken a lot for him to ask for help, but once he did, he got it. He already had their respect as an athlete, he had won a slew of trophies himself and as part of the team. He needed to win their respect again as his new self.

After the game they returned to school and finished the day. As it had only been a half day, E-Z was quite tired when Arden's Mom and his friends dropped him off after school.

After thanking them, he went inside.

"I'm home, Uncle Sam."

"I see that, did you have a good day," Sam said.

"Yes, it was a good day." He stretched and yawned.

"Come on. I have something to show you. A surprise."

"Not another one," E-Z said, as he followed his uncle down the hall. Passing first on the right, his parents' room - destined to be a guest room one day. Until then, it was exactly how they'd left it – and that's how it would stay until E-Z decided otherwise.

Every now and again Uncle Sam would offer to help him go through the room, but his nephew always said the same thing.

"I'll do it when I'm ready."

Sam reluctantly agreed. He was determined his nephew should move on. This was the first step toward that goal. Since then, he'd spoken with his counsellor who said Sam should encourage E-Z to talk more about his parents. She said making them a part of his everyday life would help him to heal more quickly. They continued along the hall, past the bathroom, and stopped at the box or storage room.

"Ta-dah!" Uncle Sam said as he pushed him in.

E-Z was speechless as he took in the newly transformed office. In the centre positioned in front of the window which looked out on the garden, was a desk. On it all set up was a brand-new gaming PC and sound system. He slid his chair under the desk – perfect fit – running his fingers along the keyboard. Nearby was a printer, stacked with paper and a garbage bin – all planned out within arm's reach.

To the left of him was a bookshelf. He rolled himself nearer. The first shelf contained books about writing and classics. He recognized several of his parents' favourites. The second contained trophies including the award for his writing. The third and fourth contained all his favourite childhood books. The bottom two shelves were empty. His eyes ran along to the top of the bookshelf, he had to back up his chair to see what was up there.

Sam came into the room beside him. He put a hand on his nephew's shoulder.

"Those, I wasn't sure if it was too soon. I…"

The pièce de résistance: a family photo. A tear rolled down his cheek as he remembered the day of the photo shoot. It was in a small photography studio downtown. They were all dressed up. Dad in his blue suit. Mom in her new blue dress with a red scarf tied around her neck. Him in his grey suit – the same one he wore for their funeral.

He fought back a sob, remembering the setup at the photographer's studio. The studio contained everything Christmassy – even though it was only July. He smiled, thinking about the cheesy Christmas decorations and fake fireplace. Weeks later, the card came with the mail, but for his parents that Christmas never arrived. He turned his chair toward the exit and made his way down the hall with his uncle trailing behind.

"I know it'll take time. I'm sorry if I went too far too soon, but it's been over a year and we, myself and your counsellor, thought it was time."

E-Z kept going. He wanted to get away. To escape to his room and shut the world out, then something occurred to him. Something crucial. His uncle couldn't have known the history of the photograph. If he had known, he wouldn't have put it there. After all he'd done for him, he owed him an explanation. He stopped.

"We never used it, it was meant for our Christmas card, but they never made it to Christmas."

"I'm so sorry. I didn't know."

"I know you didn't, but it doesn't make it hurt less."

Exhausted both physically and mentally he moved closer to his room. His interior dialogue continued with positive reinforcement. Reminding him that everything would look better in the morning. Because they almost always did.

"It was meant to be a place for you to write. Remember, you're an award-winning author now, and you have writer's blood."

He was nearly to his room – why hadn't his uncle let him get away? His temper flared.

"I wrote one short story, but it doesn't mean I can write more or want to. You say, I have Charles Dickens' blood flowing through my veins, but what I want is to be a catcher for the L.A. Dodgers. Just because they call me "tree boy" – it doesn't mean I have to settle. Why should I have to settle?"

"I wish you wouldn't let them get into your head."

"I am a tree boy! If it werent for that fricking tree!" he exclaimed as he did an abrupt turn and smacked his elbow on the wall. His not so funny, funny bone hurt like crazy.

"Are you okay?"

E-Z grunted a reply, then continued to his room. He planned to slam the door behind him. Instead, he was wedged half in and half out of the doorway. Then the wheels of his chair locked.

"FRICK!"

Sam released the chair without saying a word. Closed the door on his way out.

E-Z grabbed a few unbreakable items and tossed them against the wall. To calm himself, he visualized his parents, telling him how proud they were of him. He missed that. But, if his dad were here now, he would tell him off for being such a brat. His mother would tell him off too, but in a more kind and gentle way. He wiped the tears away. Felt the sting of shame and his body slumped down with sheer exhaustion in his wheelchair.

Uncle Sam asked through the closed door, "Are you okay?"

"Leave me alone!" E-Z replied. Even though he needed his help. Without him, he could not get into his pajamas or get into bed. He would have to sleep in the chair, in his clothes. Deep inside he always knew the truth. If he stopped caring, then everyone else would stop caring too. Then he would be truly all alone.

He wheeled his chair to the window and looked out at the night sky. Music. It had been the one thing which truly connected them as a family. Sure, they had their differences in musical genres, but when a good song came onto the radio, they put it aside.

A mangy black cat walked across the lawn. His mother had always wanted them to go to New York and see *Cats* on Broadway. He wished they would have gone together. Created a memory. Now they never would. That song, something about memories made him reach for his phone. He went for a hard rock anthem, turned up the volume. Used his fists to drum the beat on the arms of his chair as he raved and screamed out the lyrics.

Until he rocked it out so hard that he rolled out of his chair and hit the floor. At first, seeing his room from the ground up, he wanted to cry. Instead, he started laughing and couldn't stop.

"You okay in there?" Sam asked.

"Uh, I could use your help." His stomach hurt from laughing so much.

Sam's initial reaction was alarm - when he saw his nephew on the floor holding his stomach. When he realized he was holding it from laughter, he slumped down on the floor beside him.

Later, when Sam was leaving, he said, "you'll be okay, kiddo."

"We'll be okay."

That's when they made a pact to get tattoos.

CHAPTER 2

"**S**ORRY, I CAN'T PLAY baseball with you guys today."

"Come on," Arden said. "You weren't *that* bad last time."

"Get lost," E-Z replied. He picked up speed to meet his uncle and collided with Mary Garner, Head Cheerleader.

"Oh, sorry, Mary."

It was the first time he'd seen her since the accident. He looked up, as her hair dropped like a curtain over his eyes: it smelled like cinnamon and honey.

"Moron," she said. "Watch where you're going."

She backed up and marched away. Her entourage followed.

He smiled, craned his neck to watch her. His friends came alongside and did the same. Arden whistled.

She glanced over her shoulder and flipped the bird in their direction.

"God, she is fantastic," PJ said.

"She's hot," Arden said.

"Very."

Now leaving the school, PJ asked, "So, tell us why you don't want to play today."

"Yeah, help us, understand," Arden said, pulling a face and crossing his eyes. "We're useless without you."

"Look, Uncle Sam and I made a pact. To do something together - something major - after school today."

His friends crossed their arms blocking the path of his chair.

"You still intend to exclude us – and you won't even tell us why?" the red head PJ said.

"You're a total douchebag."

"We'd never do that to you."

They walked away, picking up the pace.

E-Z accelerated, but it wasn't enough. "Wait! We're getting tattoos!"

His friends stopped in their tracks.

"I'm getting a tattoo in memory of my mom and dad - dove wings, one on each shoulder."

"We're coming with you!"

"I thought you guys might think I was soppy."

They continued walking without speaking for a bit.

"Uncle Sam is meeting me at the tattoo place."

CHAPTER 3

WHEN SAM SAW HIS nephew with his friends he was surprised.

"I thought this pact was between us, i.e., a secret?"

"The guys wanted to take me to a game – I had to tell them."

"Okay, fair enough. But I'm not in the habit of standing in for their parents or giving permission on their parents' behalf." Then to PJ and Arden, "I'm okay with you two being here, but only your parents can approve your tattoos."

"Wait!" PJ said. "I never even thought about us getting tattoos."

"Mine will definitely say no," Arden said. His parents were having problems, which he took full advantage of. He acted like their constant fighting wasn't bothering him most of the time. Every now and then, when he couldn't take it anymore, he sought refuge at a friend's house.

"Mine too." PJ was the eldest and had two sisters aged five and seven. His parents encouraged him to set a good example and most of the time he did. By focusing on a future in sports, he kept himself on track.

Sharing a lightbulb moment, the teenagers high fived each other.

"What?" Sam inquired.

"We'll tell them why E-Z is doing it, and that we want tattoos to support him," PJ said.

Arden nodded.

"Wait a minute. So, you two cretins want to use the death of my parents as an excuse to get tattooed?"

Sam opened his mouth, but words escaped him.

PJ and Arden were red-faced, staring at the pavement.

E-Z let them off the hook. "Fine with me."

Sam closed his mouth as he and the two boys formed a semi-circle around the wheelchair.

"Promise me one thing though - no butterflies allowed."

"Hey, what do you guys have against butterflies?" Sam asked.

CHAPTER 4

To make a long story short, PJ and Arden convinced their parents to let them get tattoos.

"Be with you in a sec," the tattoo artist said, glancing at the four of them. Facing the mirror, was a burly male customer who was adding another tattoo to his collection of many. This new one was between his thumb and forefinger. "Are you Sam?" the man doing the tattoo asked.

Sam's stomach felt a bit queasy, as he'd read the hand was one of the most painful places to get tattooed. "Yes, I spoke with you on the phone. This is my nephew E-Z, and his friends PJ and Arden."

"All four of you want tattoos, today? Because I was only expecting two of you."

"Sorry about that. We can reschedule, if necessary, or I can have mine done on another day," Sam said wishfully.

"As luck would have it, my daughter is coming in to help me soon. So, welcome to Tattoos-R-Us. You can wait over there. Help yourself to a glass of water. There are also some brochures you might want to check out. Might help you to decide where you want your tattoo. Each area on the body has a pain threshold." The burly guy getting tattooed sniggered.

"Thanks," Sam replied as they moved toward the waiting area. Once seated on a sofa, his bouncing knee gave PJ and Arden the heebie-jeebies. They crossed the room and looked at the bulletin board. To steady his nerves, Sam blathered on. "I checked them out on the internet, they've been in business for twenty-five years, and that man we spoke to he's the owner. They have excellent standing with the Better Business Bureau. Plus, loads of five-star reviews on their website."

All eyes turned as a striking woman dressed in goth-like attire entered the premises. She was thirty-something and judging by her features the owner's daughter. She had tattoos on every bit of exposed flesh, and sporadic piercings everywhere else.

"Sorry I'm late," she said, touching her father on the shoulder. She glanced at the waiting area, whispered something to him. She beamed a toothy smile and turned toward the customers.

"Hi, I'm Josie." She held out her hand and shook hands with each of them. "That's Rocky over there. He's the owner and I'm his daughter."

"I'm Sam, and this is my nephew E-Z and his two friends, PJ and Arden." He fell rather than sat back down again.

Josie went to get him a glass of water.

E-Z was thinking about how much the piercing on her tongue must've hurt, then he said to his uncle, "You don't have to."

"Are you calling me a chicken?" he said, with his entire body shaking as Josie placed the glass into his hand. As he raised it toward his lips, he spilled some water.

"You guys are tattoo virgins, right?" Josie asked.

E-Z thought she had a sweet voice, like Stevie Nicks his father's favourite vocalist from Fleetwood Mac, singing about Rhiannon the witch.

They didn't have to answer, as their silence said it all.

"Well, you're in excellent hands with Rocky. He's the best tattoo artist in town. It'll hurt guys. Yes, it'll hurt. But it's like that kind of hurt John Cougar sings about. You know - Hurts So Good."

Sam grimaced. "How much does it actually hurt?"

"It depends on your threshold for pain – and where you choose to get it. There's a brochure over there, which maps out the various areas of the body giving a pain rating."

E-Z felt his face grow hot, and his friends' complexions had a similar hue. He glanced in Sam's direction, taking notice of his complexion which had altered to a greenish tinge.

Josie continued. "After your first tattoo, you might grow to like it and want more."

Sam stood, his body quivering with fear.

"He might need a little fresh air," E-Z said, corralling his uncle toward the door.

Once outside, Sam paced up and down the sidewalk, with his heart racing like it was going to jump out of his chest. "I wish to god I smoked."

"I appreciate your coming down here with me, I do, but honestly, you don't have to go through with it. I know we made a pact, and this is something I want to do – in memory of my mom and dad - but you don't owe me anything. Why not go for a walk, grab a coffee and we'll text you when we're finished, okay?"

"I said I'd be there for you, always. I am here for you now. I hate needles. And drills. I thought I could do it, but now I realize the fear is stronger than I am. I'm such a wuss."

"You've always been there for me, Uncle Sam. You don't have to prove it to me, to anyone, by getting a tattoo you don't even want. Now, get out of here. I'll phone you when we're finished." He wheeled himself back up the ramp with his friends falling in line behind him. He glanced over his shoulder at Sam. The poor guy was as stiff as a statue.

"I'll be okay. Now, take off."

Sam laughed. "But before I go, you'd better give me the letter I wrote last night, so I can add in PJ and Arden's names. Because without my permission – none of you are getting tattoos."

"Good thinking," E-Z said as he handed the note down the line. Now signed it came back up again. He put it into his pocket, and they went inside where Josie was waiting.

"Okay, you're next. If you're going to piss your pants, I'll show you where the toilet is now."

"Bite me," E-Z said as he wheeled his chair into position.

✳✳✳

WHILE ROCKY WAS FINISHING at the counter, Josie handed E-Z a book containing tattoos.

"I already know without looking. I'd like a dove wing, on each shoulder." There they were again, the green and yellow lights. He wanted so to bat them away, but he didn't want Josie to think he was nuts too.

Josie flipped through the book. "Are these what you had in mind?"

He nodded, then watched her in the mirror as she washed her hands, then put on a pair of black gloves. She removed ink cups from the sterile packaging and set them out on the table.

"Do you have a note, from your parent or guardian? I'm assuming you're not eighteen?"

E-Z smiled and handed her the note.

"Everything looks fine. Now to more important matters. Do you have a hairy back?" She smiled. "If you do, we'll need to clean and shave it first. I mean your entire back."

"Definitely not."

The sound of his friends sniggering from the waiting area made him smile too. Meanwhile, Josie disappeared into the back room and there was music. For a second, Another Brick in the Wall, then no music.

"Hey, why'd you do that?" he asked.

"I abhor anything by Pink Floyd." She continued setting things up.

"You can't say that, unless you've never listened to Dark Side of the Moon."

"I listened, it was crap," she said as she pulled his shirt over his head. "Oh!"

POP.

POP.

And the two lights vanished.

Rocky walked over and stood beside her. "What the heck?"

"What the heck, indeed," Josie said.

Which brought PJ and Arden over.

"I don't get it, E-Z. Why would you lie?"

"Of course, he wouldn't lie – E-Z never lies," Arden said.

"WHAT!?" E-Z asked, trying to maneuver his chair so he could see what they were seeing. "Lie? About what? Tell me, whatever it is. I can take it."

Josie asked, "Why did you lie about being a tattoo virgin?"

✳ ✳ ✳

"I DIDN'T!" E-Z STAMMERED, having no clue what she meant.

"Wait a minute," Arden said. "Come on bud, if you lied, you must have a good reason."

"The jig is up!" PJ said. "Although, he couldn't have gotten them without an adult's permission."

Rocky grabbed a hand mirror and positioned it so E-Z could see what they were seeing. Two tattoos, one on his right shoulder and the other on his left. Wings.

"What the?"

"He told me he wanted wings," Josie said. "I thought you were a nice kid."

"I am! Honestly, I have no idea how they got there, and these are not the kind of wings I wanted. I wanted dove wings. These look more like, angel wings."

"Come on mate," Rocky said. "These were done by a pro. A while ago. And they are quite exceptional angel wings. My compliments to whoever did them. Tell them if they are ever looking for a job, to see me."

"Cross my heart, I didn't get tattoos. This is the first time I have ever been in a tattoo place. Ask my uncle. He will back me up. He knows."

"None of this makes sense," Arden said.

Rocky shook his head. "At least own up to it, kid."

"Do you two want tattoos?" Josie asked with her hands on her hips.

"No," they replied.

"Men are such liars," Josie said as they closed the door behind them.

"Never mind, love, it's time we had dinner anyway," then he put the CLOSED sign on the door.

✳✳✳

SAM RETURNED TO SEE the three boys waiting outside the studio. Their body language was strange. The red head PJ had his arms crossed, while the olive-skinned Arden his hands on his hips. Meanwhile, his nephew was close to tears.

"Thank god, Uncle Sam, thank god you're back."

He rushed closer. "Oh no, was it terribly painful? It will ease up in a few days. It will be okay. Now let me have a look." He whistled as his nephew leaned forward so he could raise his shirt. "Damn those must have hurt."

"They probably did," PJ said.

"When he *first* got them."

"First? What?"

"He already had them when she took off his shirt."

"What we can't figure out is, how?"

"What do you mean? I can assure you he didn't have them yesterday."

"See, I told you Uncle Sam would back me up." If they didn't believe him, they'd believe his uncle, but why would they think he'd lie about it? They knew he wasn't a liar.

"According to Rocky, he's had these things for awhile."

"See how they're all healed up?" PJ said. "Rocky and Josie were annoyed, and they have every right to be since E-Z seemed as surprised as we were to see them."

"And you two," Sam asked, "how did your tattoos go?"

"We decided not to go ahead," PJ said.

"It didn't feel right."

Sam said, "Tell us what happened. Explain yourself man because I can't make head nor tales of it."

"I can't. Uncle Sam, you know they were not there yesterday. I have no explanation. All I want, is to go home." He started moving, strumming the wheels of his chair, faster, faster still faster. He wanted to get away, anywhere away. If they didn't believe him, then to hell with them.

As he approached the end of the street, the lights changed from green to red. A little girl on her own was already in forward momentum to cross. She stepped off the curb, as a camper van rounded the corner. His wheelchair lifted off the ground and shot toward her. He reached out, grabbed her. Just in time to save her from going under the wheels of the vehicle.

Now out of danger, the wheelchair touched back down, and he carried her to safety. In front of him, a larger than normal white swan stood. It gave him a thumb's up with its wing, then flew away.

"Swan," the little girl said, as he looked around for her parents.

E-Z took the opportunity to blend into the crowd and disappear around the corner, then he strummed the spokes of his wheels harder than he'd ever done before and soon was a few blocks away.

"Did you see that?" Arden exclaimed, coming to a stop at the corner. "Ouch," he said as the woman behind him bumped into him. "Ouch" he heard behind him, other pedestrians behind him collided.

PJ held his ground, as the guy behind barreled into him. To Arden he said, "Yeah, I saw it…but I'm not sure what I saw. The tattoo wings were one thing, this was…what? A miracle?"

"It was an optical illusion," Sam said, as his phone vibrated. It was a message from E-Z asking him to get him asap near the hardware store parking lot. "E-Z needs me, will you two be able to make your way back home again?"

"Sure, no problem, Sam."

"I hope he's okay."

Sam made his way back to the car, trying to keep his cool as he tried to logic out what he had just happened.

Neither of the boys wanted to talk about what they'd seen – E-Z's wheelchair in flight.

"Did you see that?" others whispered behind them as a crowd gathered.

"Wish I'd had my phone ready," a woman said.

A second woman with a microphone and camera pushed her way to the front. When the light changed, she crossed the road, followed by a couple, in tears – the little girls' parents. Behind them was the driver of the camper van.

"Thank god, you were there," he cried. "I didn't see her. You are a hero kid. Thank you."

"Mommy!" the child called, as her mother pulled her into her arms. She and her husband hugged her close, as the reporter moved in, and the camera operator recorded the moment.

Sobbing nearby was the man who'd nearly hit her. The reporter and photographer spoke with him. "He saved her, and me. The boy, the boy in the wheelchair."

They tried to find him, but he was gone. He was hiding out, like a criminal. Waiting for Uncle Sam to come and rescue him. Trying to make sense of what had happened. Trying not to freak out.

Back at the scene, two lights, one green and one yellow wiped the minds of everyone in the vicinity. Then they destroyed all recorded footage.

"What are we doing here?" the reporter asked.

"No idea," the camera man replied.

On the way home, E-Z kind of, felt like a hero. But he knew the real hero was the chair; his wheelchair which had taken flight.

E-Z Dickens was a Tattoo Angel.

✳✳✳

"**I** FLEW UNCLE SAM. I really flew."

Sam pulled into the driveway and parked.

"You saw it, right? You saw me rescue that little girl. I couldn't have made it on time, and my wheelchair knew it and lifted off the ground and sped toward her."

"Yes, I saw it. It was exceptional. I mean the way you saved that little girl from harm. But your chair didn't lift off. It was momentum, propelling you forward. With the adrenalin rush and how fast you had to move to get there, it felt like you were flying – but you weren't."

"I flew. The chair left the ground."

"E-Z come on. You know and I know there was no flying. You must know that. I mean, what do you think you are? A fricking angel?"

Sam got out of the car, pulled the wheelchair from the trunk, and came around to help his nephew into it. As he did, E-Z's right shoulder scraped against the edge of the door, and he cried out in pain.

"Water!" he screamed. "It feels like I'm going up in flames."

Sam ran to the kitchen and returned with a bottle of water.

E-Z dumped it on his shoulder. It eased up a little, then his other shoulder felt like it was on fire. He poured the rest of the bottle onto it. Sam pushed him into the house, while E-Z tried to rip his shirt off. Sam helped him pull it over his head.

"Oh no!" Sam shouted, covering his nose. His nephew's shoulder blades now looked and smelled like charred barbecue meat. He hurried into the kitchen for more water.

On the way E-Z screamed and kept on screaming, until he blacked out.

CHAPTER 5

I T WAS DARK AND he was all alone, with only the shadow from the moon spreading above him across the sky.

His arms were crossed upon his chest, like he'd seen dead bodies positioned at an open casket funeral. He shook them out. Now relaxed he deposited them on the arm rests of his wheelchair only to discover he wasn't in it. Frightened he'd topple over; he re-crossed his arms over his chest. But wait, he didn't keel over when he uncrossed them before - he did it again and remained upright.

E-Z kept one arm firmly against his chest, while the other, his right, reached out as far as it would go. His fingertips connected with something cool and metallic. With his left arm he did the same, finding again metal. Leaning forward, he touched the wall in front of him, and did the same behind him. As he moved around, the seat under him shifted, with give and take like a suspension system. It was this system, which was keeping him upright, or was it?

PFFT.

The sound of mist, surging into the air. Warm, it heightened his sense of smell, bathing him in a bouquet of lavender and citrus.

He descended into a deep sleep, in which he dreamed dreams which were not dreams for they were memories. The accident – it was happening all over again – looping. He threw his head back and howled.

"One moment, please," a woman's voice said.

It was a robotic voice like one heard on a recording when no human was about.

Too afraid to nod off again he asked, "Who's there? Please. Where am I?"

"You are here," the voice said, then giggled. The laughter pinged off the silo-like container, pounding his ears as it came and went.

When it stopped, he decided to break himself out. Using every bit of strength, he extended his arms and pushed. It felt good. Doing something, anything – at first – until claustrophobia had the upper hand.

PFFT.

The spray, nearer this time went straight into his eyes. The citric acid stung, and tears welled up like he'd been chopping an onion, and he stood up.

Wait a minute...

He fell back down again. He wriggled his toes. He did it again. He stretched out his right leg. Then his left leg. They worked. His legs worked. He lifted himself...

A voice, male this time said, "Please remain seated."

He pinched himself on the right thigh then on the left. Who knew a pinch or two could feel so good? No one could stop him. While he had the use of his legs, he would stand again.

There was a noise above him, like an elevator moving. The sound grew louder. He looked up. The silo ceiling was coming down. Getting bigger and bigger. Finally, it came to a full stop.

"Be seated," the male voice demanded.

E-Z raised himself up, but the ceiling inched down – until he could no longer stand. He sat patiently, waiting for the thing to retract like an elevator rising to the top – but it didn't budge.

PFFT.

"Let me out!"

"Add laudanum," the woman's voice said.

The walls paused, then sprayed out an extra-long dose.

PPPFFFTTT.

It was the last sound he heard.

✳✳✳

BACK IN HIS BED – wondering if he'd lost his mind and imagined the entire silo incident was E-Z. It felt real, it smelled real. And the two voices – why didn't they show themselves? He scratched his head, seeing two lights in front of his eyes. As before, one was green, and one was yellow.

"Hello?" he whispered, as a high-pitched whine like a scourge of mosquitoes assaulted him. He launched his right hand back, striking out with a powerful wallop. But before it connected, he froze, hand in mid-air. His eyes glazed over, like a hypnotized chicken.

POP.

POP.

The lights transformed into two creatures. Each pushed a shoulder, and E-Z dropped onto the pillow where he closed his eyes and slept.

"We should do it now, beep-beep," the former yellow light said.

"Let's make sure he's asleep, first, zoom-zoom," the former green light said.

"Okay, let's get down to work, beep-beep."

"Have we his consent, zoom-zoom?"

"He said he would, but he doesn't remember. I'm worried it's not a binding agreement. It might only be a partial, and *you-know-who* hates partials. Not to mention, the human partials would be caught betwixt and between beep-beeps."

"Yes, I like him too much to let him become a betwixt and betweener zoom-zoom."

"Like has nothing to do with it. Don't forget what happened to the swan. Not to mention – why do humans say what not to mention before they mention what they do not want to say?" Without waiting for an answer. "We'd be in a pickle and *you-know-who* would be very cross beep-beep."

"But the human already has his tattooed wings. Trials don't begin, until the subject has agreed." She snapped her fingers and a book appeared. She fluttered her wings creating a breeze which turned the pages. "See here, it says wings are only installed AFTER the subject has been approved. So, when he said yes, that must've sealed the deal zoom-zoom." She raised her arms, and the book flew up, like it was going to hit the ceiling but instead it disappeared through it.

They flew, one landed on E-Z's shoulder and one on his head.

"I didn't do it," he said, without opening his eyes.

"Sleep more, zoom-zoom," she said touching his eyes.

"Shhhh, beep-beep."

"Mom come back. Please come back!"

"He's very restless, zoom-zoom."

"He's dreaming, beep-beep."

E-Z opened his mouth and snored like a baby elephant. The breeze kept them aloft – no need to flap their wings. They giggled, until he closed his mouth. Sending them into freefall. By flapping furiously, they quickly recovered.

"Oh no, he's grinding his teeth, beep-beep."

"Humans have strange habits, zoom-zoom."

"This human child has been through enough. By administering these rights, he'll feel less pain, beep-beep."

The first creature flew onto E-Z's chest and landed, with its chin thrust forward and hands on his hips. The creature turned once, clockwise. Spinning faster, from the flutter of his wings a song emanated. The song was a low moan. A sad song from the past in celebration of a life that was no more. The creature leaned back, head resting against E-Z's chest. The spinning stopped but the song continued playing.

The second creature joined in, doing the same ritual, while turning anti-clockwise. They created a new song, minus the beep-beeps and zoom-zooms. For when they sang, onomatopoeia was not required. Whereas in everyday conversation with humans it was. This song overlaid the other and became a joyful, high-pitched celebration. An ode for things to come, of a life yet unlived. A song for the future.

A spray of diamond dust burst from their golden eye sockets. They turned in perfect synchronicity. The diamond dust sprayed from their eyes onto E-Z's sleeping body. The exchange continued, until it covered him with diamond dust from head to toe.

The teenager continued sleeping soundly. Until the diamond dust pierced his flesh – then he opened his mouth to scream but no sound emanated.

"He's waking up, beep-beep."

"Lift him, zoom-zoom."

Together they raised him up as he opened his glazed-over eyes.

"Sleep more, beep-beep."

"Feel no pain, zoom-zoom."

Cradling his body, the two creatures accepted his pain into themselves.

"Rise up, beep-beep," he commanded.

And the wheelchair, raised up. And, positioning itself under E-Z's body, it waited. When a droplet of blood descended, the chair caught it. Absorbed it. Consumed it – like it was a living thing.

As the chair's power increased, it also gained strength. Soon the chair could hold its master in mid-air. This allowed the two creatures to complete their task. Their task of joining the chair and the human. Binding them, for all eternity with the power of diamond dust, blood, and pain.

As the teenager's body shook, the punctures on his skin healed. The task was complete. The diamond dust was a part of his essence. Thus, the music came to a stop.

"It is done. Now he is bullet-proofed. And he has super strength, beep-beep."

"Yes, and it is good, zoom-zoom."

The wheelchair returned to the floor, and the teenager onto his bed.

"He will have no memory of it, but his real wings will begin functioning very soon beep-beep."

"What about the other side effects? When will they begin, and will they be noticeable zoom-zoom?"

"That I do not know. He may have physical changes...it's a risk worth taking to reduce the pain, beep-beep."

"Agreed zoom-zoom."

Exhausted, the two creatures snuggled into E-Z's chest and fell asleep. Not knowing they were there, when he stretched in the morning – they fell onto the floor.

"Oops, sorry," he said to the winged creatures before he turned over and went back to sleep.

$$* * *$$

"Are you awake?" Sam asked, before opening the door a sliver. His nephew was snoring away, but his chair wasn't where he'd left it when he helped him into bed. He shrugged and returned to his room where he read a few chapters of David Copperfield. Hours later he returned to his nephew's room.

"Knock, knock."

"Uh, good morning," E-Z said.

"Okay if I come in?"

"Sure."

"Did you sleep well?"

"I think so." He stretched then leaned back against the headboard.

"How did your chair get over here? I thought I parked it against the wall."

He shrugged.

"And look at the armrests – did you paint them?"

He leaned over, saw the red tinge, again he shrugged. "What happened to me?"

"You passed-out. What I don't understand is why. You said you felt like your shoulders were on fire. I searched online using your description and a homeopathic remedy popped up. Amazing what you can find on there. I mixed up some lavender oil with water and aloe in a spray bottle, then pumped it straight onto your skin. They said it would give you immediate relief. They weren't kidding because you relaxed and fell asleep."

"Thanks, I feel much better now." He tried to get out of bed, but the zzzzzs flew around in his head like he was Wile E. Coyote. "I think I'll stay in bed for a while longer."

"Good idea. Can I get you anything?"

"Some toast? With strawberry jam?"

"Sure kiddo." He left the room, saying he'd be back shortly. When he returned with food on a tray, his nephew tried to eat but could not hold anything down.

"Maybe just some water."

Sam brought a bottle, which E-Z attempted to drink from, even that he could not keep down.

"Think I'll continue to rest." His eyes remained open, staring ahead at nothing. "What time is it?"

"It's 5 a.m. and today is Saturday. You've been out for twelve hours. You scared me."

The connection, lavender in both places struck E-Z as strange. Had he experienced a real life cross-over? It was too much of a coincidence, that's if the silo really existed. Or had it been a dream? More like a nightmare. But his legs did work inside that metal container. He'd go back in a minute – take any risk – to gain the use of his legs again.

"E-Z?"

"Uh, what? I. Honestly, think I'd like to close my eyes and rest a little more."

Sam left the room, closing the door behind him.

E-Z drifted in and out of consciousness, while the accident played on loop. Wearing white wings, Stevie Nicks supplied the accompanying soundtrack. While in the background two lights – one green and one yellow bounced up and down.

✳✳✳

FOR THE NEXT FEW days, he tried to put the pieces together in his mind by making a list of commonalities:

White wings – white wings tattooed onto his shoulders. Stevie Nicks had white wings in his dream.

Lavender – Uncle Sam used lavender and aloe to sooth the burns. In the silo, lavender spritzed the air to calm him.

Yellow and green lights. He saw them after the accident and in his room.

Wheelchair – had flown so he could save the little girl. When he was catcher, his butt had left the chair so he could catch the ball.

Armrests – were now red. No similar incidents. No explanation.

Burning sensation on shoulders/tattoos appearing on shoulders. No explanation.

He did not believe in god anymore, not since the accident. No god would let a tree crush his parents. They were good people, never hurt anyone. What happened to his legs was beside the point. Any god worth anything, would have reached out and stopped it before it happened.

Unless maybe if there was a god, he was out for lunch. Yeah, right.

Changes were happening to his body, and he wanted answers. Deep inside he knew the only way he was going to get them was to go back into the damned silo – if it existed.

CHAPTER 6

NEXT MORNING E-Z WAS hovering in the air above his bed since his wings had sprouted. En-route to look at his new appendages in the wardrobe mirror, he nearly crashed into the wall.

"Everything okay in there?" Sam called from his room next door.

"Yes," he said, flitting sideways, as he admired his newfound power of flight. The feathery plumes fascinated him. Especially the way they propelled him forward, like they were at one with his body. Feeling more like a bird than an angel, he tried to remember what he learned in school about ornithology. He knew most birds had primary feathers, possibly ten. Without the primaries, they couldn't fly. He had more than ten primary feathers on his wings, and more secondaries too. He tried veering left, then right, assessing his maneuverability. Feeling weightless, he flitted around his room. Hovered over the wheelchair – which he no longer needed. With these wings he could soar across the world. Placing his hands on his hips, like Superman, he pointed himself in the direction of the door. He arrived there as Sam opened it.

"You scared me half to death!" Sam said, nearly jumping out of his skin.

Caught off guard, the teenager attempted to keep control of the situation. He changed direction, intending to go to the bed. The transition though, was not as easy as he'd hoped, and he went into freefall.

Sam ran for the wheelchair, moving it back and forth to keep it underneath his nephew.

E-Z recovered and went up again.

"You come down here, right now!" Sam cried; brandishing is fists in the air.

He flew toward the bed and made a safe landing. His wings closed like a music-less accordion. "That was so much fun. I can't wait to fly to school."

Sam fell into his nephew's chair. "What was that all about? And do you really think you could fly those things to school? You'd be a laughingstock."

"They'd get used to it and instead of calling me "tree boy" – they could call me fly boy. Yeah, I like that."

"From what I saw, it was an inept attempt. And fly boy sounds ridiculous."

"It was my first try. I'll get the knack of it."

Sam shook his head as curiosity got the best of him and overtook his emotions to flee.

"May I have a closer look? I mean without you taking off?" he asked standing up as E-Z turned his body toward him. "They're gone. Completely. I mean the tattoos. They've been replaced by real wings – and you can fly. Oh boy!" He sat down before he fell.

"I woke up, the wings came out and the next thing I knew, I was flying."

"It's magic. Must be. Or maybe we're dreaming, you're in my dream or I'm in yours and soon we're going to wake up and..." Sam was trying to keep calm for his nephew's sake but inside his heart was racing.

"It's no dream."

"How did they pop out? Did you have to say something? I mean, are there magic words you have to say?"

"I don't remember saying anything. Guess I could try it though." He thought about it for a few seconds, striking a pose like Rodin's Thinker. "Wait a minute, let me try something." He swished the air in a wand-less motion, "Autem!"

"When did you learn Latin?"

"There's a free app on my phone."

"Me too, I'm learning French. Try en haut."

"En haut!" Still nothing. "Lift me up! Qui exaltas me!" Annoyed he crossed his arms. "I guess it's a good thing you walked in and saw me flying, otherwise, you wouldn't believe me!" He wondered what PJ and Arden were up to – he hadn't seen them in days. Next thing he knew his wings opened and he was hovering above his bed.

"Ro-ro," Sam said, as the wings retracted, and E-Z hit the floor.

"That would have been a cool time for you to grab my chair."

Sam smiled. "Easier said than done. Sorry. Are you okay?"

"I'm not hurt. I mean physically, but mentally, who knows?" He laughed. "Mind giving me a hand into my chair?"

Sam lifted him up, deposited him safely in the chair. When he leaned back, the wings instead of retracting all the way, sprung back out in full force. Up E-Z went, flitting around like Tinkerbell.

"So, that's how it is, eh?" Sam said.

"I need to get the hang of it – not sure why – but..."

"Well, when you're ready, come on down and we'll go out for breakfast. I'll bring my laptop and we can do some research."

"Uh, that's a clever idea. We could go to Ann's Cafe. And I *would* come down – if I could." The wings retracted when E-Z was directly over his wheelchair. "Now that's what I call service," he said as he gently dropped into the chair.

They chatted, while he dressed. Then E-Z went to the bathroom, while Sam got ready.

As they made their way out of the house and toward Ann's Café, E-Z was of two minds. One, that he missed going there and two, "I haven't been there in ages. Not since..."

"I know, kiddo. Are you sure it's not too soon?"

Breakfast at Ann's Café had been a tradition for his family. Besides opening early at 6 a.m. it was within walking distance. Inside were private booths, decked out in faux leather with red checkered tablecloths. His dad always said the place had a 'far out' theme. Sixties music played on the jukeboxes – they had it rigged up, so people didn't have to pay. And posters of Marilyn Monroe, James Dean and Marlon Brando filled the walls. The menu was huge with everything from Club Sandwiches to Cheeseburgers to Fondues. But his personal favourites were the extra thick shakes and Apple Pancakes.

As soon as she saw them, owner Ann came right over. "I've missed you." She threw her arms around him.

"This is my Uncle Sam, Ann." They shook hands. "Thanks for the card and flowers by the way, it was very thoughtful."

Her eyes filled with tears. "Now, come on over here. I have the perfect table for you."

It was in a quiet corner, so he didn't have to worry about his chair getting in the way of the kitchen staff or patrons.

"I'll get your usual dish cooking straight away. Know what you'd like, Sam, or should I come back?"

"What are you having?"

"Apple Pancakes a la mode. They are the best on the planet and Ann always brings extra syrup and cinnamon."

"That sounds good, but I think I'll go for boring bacon and eggs, with a side of mushrooms."

"Got it," Ann said. "And are you going for a chocolate thick shake?" He nodded. "Coffee for you Sam? "

"Black," he replied. "And thanks for making me so welcome."

"Any Uncle of E-Z is welcome here."

After Ann went to get the drinks, he blurted out, "Uncle Sam, I think I'm turning into an angel."

"You'd have to die first," he said, as Ann placed the drinks on the table and went back toward the kitchen.

"Maybe I did die, in the car accident. For a few minutes. Who knows how long it takes to become an angel? In the movies if you get to the Pearly Gates, the big man can turn things around and send you right back down here again. That's if you believe in such things—which I don't."

"Me either. There are no such things as angels. Nor devils. Other than inside of each one of us. I mean we all have good, and we all have bad in us. It's what makes us humans. As to the dying, they would have told me if they had to resuscitate you. They said nothing of the sort."

"Then, how do explain the sudden appearance of the tattoos, and now they've turned into real wings? I didn't have them yesterday. So, what happened between yesterday and today? Nothing to warrant the growth of any new appendages."

"Not that you can think of," Sam said. He laughed.

E-Z stabbed a pancake and stuffed it into his mouth, letting the syrup run down his chin. Ann made herself scarce.

"Well, you certainly don't look very angelic at the moment," Sam said, picking up a forkful of scrambled eggs. "Mm, these are really good." After a few more bites, he reached into his briefcase and pulled out his laptop. He clicked it on and typed in "define angel." He turned the screen so they could read the information while eating.

"A messenger, especially of god," Sam read, "a person who performs a mission of god or acts as if sent by god."

"Acts as if," E-Z repeated as he stuffed more pancakes into his mouth.

Sam read, "An informal person, especially a woman, who is kind, pure or beautiful. You are quite pretty, with your blond hair and blue eyes."

"Shut up."

"A conventional representation," he paused. " Of any of these beings depicted in human form with wings." Sam took another sip of coffee, in time for Ann to refill his cup.

"You guys will get indigestion, reading and eating at the same time."

E-Z laughed.

Sam said, "No, I'm in I.T., so I'm pretty good at multitasking."

Ann sniggered and walked away.

"What do they mean by, 'these beings?'" E-Z asked.

"It says in medieval angelology, angels were divided into ranks. Nine orders: seraphim, cherubim, thrones, dominations (also known as dominions)," he paused, took a sip of water. Then continued, "Virtues, principalities (also known as princedoms), archangels, and angels."

"Whoa! Try saying those ten times quickly." He smiled. "I had no idea there were so many kinds of angels."

"Me either. This food is so good, I keep wondering if you and I are dreaming."

"You mean you wish we were dreaming – and my wings would disappear?"

"They could leave as quickly as they came." He moved the laptop closer and typed in "Human grows angel wings." E-Z scoffed but leaned in closer to see what popped up. Sam clicked on a scientific article.

"Like I said, no evidence of angel wings on record. I didn't think so. I think that incident, you know when I saved the little girl—had something to do with them—appearing. It was a trigger because the burning started right after I got home and then, well you know the rest."

"How are you two doing here?" Ann asked.

"I've ordered you two more pancakes, E-Z, As usual. Unless you can eat more?"

"Perfect."

"And what about you, Sam?"

"Just a refill," he said, offering up his empty mug which she took away and came back with filled to the brim. A bell rang in the kitchen, and she went to retrieve the pancakes.

E-Z dumped maple syrup onto them, followed by a dob of butter. "You're the greatest," he said to Ann. She smiled and left them to finish their meals.

Uncle Sam watched his nephew intently. He wished he'd ordered the Apple Pancakes, but he was already full.

"What?"

"I don't know, it's like when you taste the food, your face lights up like an angel on a Christmas tree."

E-Z put his fork down. "Very funny. You're a regular comedian."

When they'd finished eating, Sam asked, "So after reading about angels, have you changed your mind? I mean do you still think you're turning into one. And if yes, what are you going to do about it?"

"What do you mean, DO? I have wings, might as well use them."

"The way I see it is, if you don't use them, if you deny their very existence – then they'll go away."

E-Z shook his head. "Not an option. You saw what happened. They came out, without me doing anything and I told you, when I woke up this morning I was flying above my bed. I was fricking HOVERING."

"E-Z, I'm thinking of the future. Maybe you need to speak to someone, we need to speak to someone about this."

"The accident happened over a year ago, the counsellor said I'm fine. Besides, this is all new."

"It could be delayed. Something might have triggered it."

"Let's go over the facts. Number one, I had tattoos when I didn't get tattoos. Number two, my chair lifted off the ground and I saved a little girl – plus, I lifted off my seat to catch a ball at a game. I was in denial about that until recently... Number three the tattoos burned like hell. Number four, real wings appeared. Number five, I can fly. Any of that sound familiar to you? I mean in other instances."

"That's what I don't understand. How this could happen, but the mind is an enormously powerful computer. It's what separates us from the animal kingdom and why man has survived for so long. I've heard stories, where a person was in extreme danger and help arrived. Or, where a person was trapped under a vehicle – and a passerby was able to lift the car to save their life."

"I read about that; it's called hysterical strength – but I've never heard of a case when wings grew."

"Maybe the wings, appeared, to save you."

"From what? Too much sleep?" he laughed. "They would have been nice at the accident. I could have flown mom and dad to get help instead of waiting there with a bloody log on me. Holding me down. It's no miracle. I, don't know what it is Uncle Sam, all I know is that it is."

"We're chatting. Assessing. Exchanging ideas. Trying to find answers."

"It would be nice to have answers, but...who would be an expert we could ask in this situation?"

"What about a minister or a priest?"

E-Z shook his head. He hadn't been in a church since his parents' funeral.

"What do we have to lose?"

"I guess it's worth a shot, but. Oh, oh."

"What is it?"

"I feel pushing against my shoulder blades. I've got to go, and we didn't drive here. Sorry I've got to hurry. See you at home." He sped out of the café and kept on going, until his wings burst out of his hoodie, and he lifted off the ground. At home he realized he didn't have a key, but he couldn't remain on the front porch – not with the wings out. He tried Latin to get them to go back in – but nothing worked. So, he flew up and managed to get in through his bedroom window without being seen by anyone.

"E-Z!" Sam called when he arrived home. "E-Z!"

"I'm up here."

"Are you okay? I got here as quickly as I could."

"Come on in, take a seat. No sign of them retracting – yet."

Seeing the open window. "I take it you flew up here?"

"Yeah, good thing I forgot to lock my window last night. We might as well continue our discussion, until I can go out again."

"I know a priest. If anyone can help, he can."

Two hours later, with tunes blasting out of the radio they were on the way to see the priest. Hozier's Take Me to Church filled the airwaves. Coincidence? They thought not and sang along to the lyrics at the top of their voices. Thankfully with the windows up no one could hear them.

***

AT THE CHURCH THERE was no wheelchair access and lots of stairs to climb.

"You head over under the shade of the big oak tree, and I'll go and find Father Hopper," Sam suggested.

"Is that his real name?" E-Z laughed.

"As far as I know. You stay put and I'll be right back."

"Will do."

The teenager took out his phone. Although he enjoyed the shade provided by the tree – it made it impossible to see his screen. He repositioned his chair, taking notice of an unusual hum in the air. A noise, which seemed to be coming from the tree itself.

He looked up, trying to discern if it was a bird, when the pitch rose, and the volume increased. He muted his phone. The sound ended, and a new sound began. This one was melodic; mesmerizing and he fell into a dreamlike state.

His head lolled forward, until a new sound jarred him awake. Whispers, coming from above his head. Voices flowing from the tree's foliage. He crossed his arms, as a chill went through him, causing his wings to burst free. Before he knew it, his chair lifted off the ground. He ducked branches as he rose into the heart of the massive oak tree.

"Put me down!" he commanded.

He continued rising. As his limbs connected with the tree, blood dripped down his forearms and head.

"Stop! You stupid..."

"That's not very nice, beep-beep," a wee high-pitched voice said.

"I thought you said he was lovely when he was awake zoom-zoom," a second voice said.

"Whoa!" E-Z said, trying to get a grip and avoid completely wigging out. He took a few deep breaths. Calmed himself. "Who, what and where are you?"

"Who are we indeed, beep-beep."

Once again, the same lights, green and one yellow danced before his eyes.

Curious, he said, "Hi."

The yellow light disappeared.

A scream.

Then the green one vanished.

"What the? You two, whatever you are, cut that out. You owe me an explanation. I know you've been stalking me. Come out and face me!"

POP.

A tiny green angel-like thing landed on his nose. A strangely unappealing, almost limburger-ish stink wafted in his direction. He covered his nose.

"Good-day, E-Z, beep-beep," the thing said, with a bow.

When it said his name, he lost control of his wings. He wobbled and swayed in mid-air like a bird learning to fly. He willed his wings to come back out again, but they ignored him. He clung to the arms of his chair as he plummeted.

POP!

Now there were two of them. Each grabbed one of his ear's and lowered him and his chair safely to the ground.

"Ouch," E-Z said rubbing his ears as the priest and his uncle came around the corner. "Uh, thanks, I think."

POP.

POP.

The two creatures disappeared.

"E-Z, this is Father Bradley Hopper and he's keen to help."

Hopper extended his hand, E-Z did the same. As their flesh connected, the teenager disappeared.

Hopper and Sam remained side by side, with their eyes glazed over. Both were staring into nothingness like two mannequins in a shop window.

CHAPTER 7

E-Z'S FEET TOUCHED DOWN on the ground and at first, he was blinded by white. He put one foot in front of the other, first walking, then jogging on the spot, then breaking into a full run. He threw himself into the wall, bouncing, like he was in a jumping castle.

POP

POP

He was no longer alone. In front of him were two multi-winged things, in flowers. One was green, the other yellow. As he drew nearer, their wings, turned like a kaleidoscope around golden eyes.

He touched the petal-wings of the green flower first. He'd never seen a fully green flower before, let alone one with eyes. The eyes he recognized from their meeting before. The wings tickled his finger and the green flower laughed. He avoided getting too close with his nose, expecting a cheesy smell to waft forward – but it didn't.

The second flower, yellow, had more petal-wings than the other. The petals responded to his touch, like coral moving in the ocean. The golden eyes on this one, had defined eyelashes. He leaned in, to take a closer look.

As he continued observing the two, a PFFT filled the air. With it a powerful and most sickly-sweet stench came forth making him feel queasy. He backed away, covering his nose, and wiping the sting from his eyes.

The yellow flower spoke. "My name is Reiki and we brought you here beep-beep."

"Where exactly is here? And why are my legs working?"

"It matters not where, E-Z Dickens, nor why you are as you are beep-beep."

He crossed the room and picked up the yellow flower with his right hand and the green with his left. WHOOSH! This time a pungent mist hit him, and he started sneezing and kept on sneezing.

"Please put us down, before you drop us, beep-beep."

"There's a box of tissues, over there zoom-zoom."

"Oh, sorry." He put them down, picked up a tissue – but he no longer needed it. He held the distance, leaning his back against a white wall.

"We brought you here now, beep-beep."

"I'm Hadz, by the way zoom-zoom."

"Because you needed to know beep-beep."

"That you must not speak to the priest, about your wings zoom-zoom."

"In fact, you must not speak to anyone about anything beep-beep."

Putting his hand on the wall, he walked, thinking as he did. "First of all, why are you saying beep-beep and zoom-zoom?"

Reiki and Hadz rolled their eyes. "Haven't you heard of onomatopoeia?"

"Of course, I have."

"Then you should know, beep-beep."

"That it adds excitement, action and interest, zoom-zoom."

"To ensure the reader hears and remembers, beep-beep."

"What you want them to know, zoom-zoom."

He laughed. "That's true if you're reading something, but not necessary in conversation. I remember what Reiki says because he says it and I remember what Hadz says because she says it. I'm assuming one of you is a girl and one is a boy – is that correct?"

"Yes," Hadz confirmed. "I'm a girl. Whew, I'm glad I don't have to keep saying zoom-zoom."

"And I'm a boy. I'll miss saying beep-beep."

"You can say them if you want to, but it's a bit annoying and during conversation the repetition can be boring."

"We don't want to be boring!"

"It would defeat our purpose, for bringing you here."

"Okay," E-Z said. "So, now let's get back to what you said before we started talking about a literary device." They nodded. "If I can't tell anyone about what's happening to me, then I'm alone in this thing - whatever it is. I saved a little girl. I'm assuming it had something to do with you?"

"Yes, you are correct in that assumption beep, oops, sorry."

"I want to know what this is and why it's happening to me?"

"Close your eyes," Hadz said.

"I will, but no funny business."

The flowers giggled.

His feet left the ground, and he landed in a different room. In this room, like before he was at first blinded by white. As his eyes became accustomed to his surroundings, he noticed the books. Shelves and shelves stacked with volumes sky high.

"Don't be afraid," Hadz said.

He wasn't afraid. In fact, he was ecstatic. Because in this room, not only could he use his legs, but he could feel the blood pulsing through them. His senses heightened; the old book smell wafted in his direction. He sniffed in the sweet prunus dulcis (sweet almond) perfume. Blended with planifolia (vanilla) it created a perfect anisole. His heart beating, blood pumping – he never felt more alive. He wanted to stay, forever.

Inside his shoes, the movement of each toe gave him pleasure. He remembered a game he used to play with as a little boy. He removed his shoes and socks and touched each toe saying the rhyme, "This little piggy went to market."

"He's lost his mind," Reiki said, as E-Z exclaimed, "Wee!"

"Give him a moment. This is a pretty amazing place."

E-Z put his socks back on. He slid around the room on the white floors which were shiny like a sheet of ice. He laughed, as he propelled himself into the first, then second wall, bouncing and landing on the floor. He couldn't stop laughing, until he noticed something strange going on with the books above him. He shook his head when one flew off the shelf into his hand. It was a book by his ancestor, Charles Dickens. The book opened by itself, fanned through from start to finish, then flew back up to where it came from.

"Welcome to the angel library," Reiki said.

"Wow! Just wow! So, you two are angels, then?"

"You are correct," Hadz said. "And you are here, because we have been appointed as your mentors."

"Appointed? Appointed by who? God?" he scoffed.

Hadz and Reiki looked at each other, shaking their floral heads.

"Our purpose."

"Is to explain your mission to you."

"Also, to show you the way. To assist you," they said together.

"Mission? What mission?" His mind drifted off. In his head he heard the theme from Mission Impossible. Saw Tom Cruise being cable dropped into a computer room. "Hey. Wait a minute! You two were in my room, weren't you? And you've been following me since the accident."

"We were waiting for the right time to introduce ourselves," Reiki said. "We had hoped to do it in a less formal way, but when you were...."

"...Going to speak with the Priest, we had to press forward."

"Well, you sure took your time. I thought I was hallucinating," he said more loudly than he'd wanted to.

POP.

Reiki disappeared.

"Now look what you've done!" Hadz said.

POP.

As they were gone and he had no idea where, when or if they'd get back. Still, he wasn't going to waste a minute. He hit the floor and did twenty push-ups, followed by the same number of jumping jacks. His eyes smarted from the glare and he wished he had some sunglasses.

TICK-TOCK.

A pair of sunglasses appeared out of thin air. He put them on, as his stomach growled. He took a selfie, then checked the time. Something weird was happening with the clock. It was going crazy. And the numbers never stopped changing. His stomach growled again.

TICK-TOCK.

A cheeseburger and fries appeared, now his hands were full. He thought of a chocolate thick shake with a maraschino cherry on top.

TICK-TOCK.

An extra-large shake, with a cherry on the top arrived on a white table which hadn't been there before. Or had it? Perhaps he hadn't noticed since they both were white.

Before he began to eat, he savored the smell of it, then with each bite, the flavour. It was like he'd never eaten a cheeseburger or fries before. And the cherry, tasted so sweet, followed by the chocolatey chocolate. He devoured his meal standing up. Food always tasted better when consumed standing. This order tasted so good; it was ridiculous.

When he finished, he thanked no one for the meal. Then turned his attention to the library and, a white ladder which he hadn't noticed before. Just thinking of it was enough to make the ladder move closer to him, like it wanted to be of use. He climbed aboard, and it moved, like a disc on a Ouija board, passing by shelf after shelf of books. Then, it stopped.

As he climbed, he read the titles on the spines. Those directly in front of him were by Charles Dickens, each volume had its own pair of wings.

One flew toward him, *A Christmas Carol*. It flipped through a couple of pages, to show him that it was a First Edition, published on December 19, 1843. As it continued moving the pages, he marveled at the illustrations. How detailed they were and in full colour too. And in the background, behind Tiny Tim and his family on one of the drawings, something moved. Eyes. Two pairs. Hadz and Reiki! He nearly dropped the book. Since it had wings it went back to where it lived on the shelf. Meanwhile he lost his balance, dropped down the ladder and hung on for dear life. When he was stable again, he came down gradually and planted his feet firmly on the ground. He wondered why his wings hadn't sprung forth to help him. Everything else had wings here that worked, in fact the angels had multiple pairs of wings. In the world out there, his legs did not work, and he had wings, which did. Here, wherever he was, his legs did work, but his wings were now defunct.

He scratched his head. If only Uncle Sam was here. And yet, he couldn't talk to him. It was forbidden. But why? What could they do to him? The angels had been stalking him since the accident. He assumed they were good angels, since they hadn't hurt him – yet. Homesickness rushed upon him like a giant wave, threatening to take him under.

"I want to go home!" he shouted, as his phone vibrated. Before he had the chance to unlock it...

POP.

Reiki grabbed it and tossed it to...

POP.

Hadz who threw it against the furthest white wall. It bounced, hit the floor, and shattered into bits.

"You owe me four hundred dollars for a new phone! I hope you angels have cash."

Hadz reached over and slapped E-Z across the face with his wing. The feathers tickled, instead of hurting him. "Now you, E-Z Dickens, you sit down here." A white chair pressed against the back of his legs forcing him to sit.

"And stop being a dick," Reiki said.

"Whoa! Can angels say that? What kind of angels are you anyway? Angels in training? Am I the guy who is going to help you to earn your wings?"

He realized they already had wings. In fact, several pairs of them. So, the point he was trying to make seemed moot as they hovered above him.

"Am I the guy who is going to help you, or are you meant to be helping me? Because if you are, which you said you were, then you are doing a terrible job. I won't be putting in a good word for either of you anytime soon."

"We are waiting for an apology."

"Well, you'll be waiting for it, for a long time. Because I'm thirsty."

TICK-TOCK.

A mug of root beer in a frosted glass appeared. He downed it in one gulp. "Because you brought me here, without my consent. And..."

"SHUT UP!" a booming voice said, as she enfolded from one of the white walls.

She was as tall as the ceiling. In fact, taller. She was crooked, yet immense in size and stature. Her wings brushed against the walls and the ceiling. "HOLD YOUR TONGUE!" the over-sized angel demanded, pulling her wings toward E-Z with a SWOOSH until he was right up in his face.

✳︎✳︎✳︎

"E-Z DICKENS, YOU HAVE been summoned here before me," the huge angel said. "I am Ophaniel, ruler of the moon and stars. And these, are my underlings. You SHALL NOT treat them with insolence. You SHALL treat them with kindness and respect for they are my EYES and my EARS to you. Without them you are NOTHING."

He stammered out an unintelligible sentence fighting back the urge to flee.

"DO NOT interrupt until I finish speaking," Ophaniel commanded.

He nodded, body shaking, too afraid to say a word.

"E-Z," his voice thundered. "You have been saved. We have saved you, for a purpose."

Reiki and Hadz flittered closer and sat upon Ophaniel's shoulders.

"Be still," Ophaniel commanded.

They folded their wings, leaning in so as not to miss a word.

E-Z made a mental note to ask them how to fold up his wings as efficiently as they did theirs. That's if he got his wings back.

Ophaniel continued. "When your parents died E-Z Dickens, you, also should have died. It was your destiny. One that we altered for our purpose. We successfully pleaded your case. We promised you'd do remarkable things. That you'd help others. We saved you, and a debt was owed. A debt most of which you paid in full by surrendering your legs."

Surrendered? That sounded like he had a choice. That he'd made the final decision never to walk again which was a lie. He opened his mouth to speak, but Ophaniel's voice thundered on.

"There is still a debt owed, a debt you owe to us."

E-Z took in a big gulp of air. He wanted to speak but couldn't. His lips moved but no sound came forth. How dare this, angel, make decisions for him and tell him a debt is owed?

"We gave you tools – a powerful chair. This to help you. So, that one day you may be here with your parents and walk with us, with them, in the evermore." Ophaniel hesitated for a few seconds, to let that sink in. "You may ask me one question today, but only one. Make it good."

Instead of contemplating his question, E-Z blurted out, "When will I get to see my parents again?"

"When you have paid your debt in full."

"One more question, please."

"There will be time for questions and there will be time for answers. For now, you are in the care of my underlings. You may ask them questions and they may choose to answer. Or they may choose not to. It will be their choice to answer yay or nay. In the same way you will have a choice whether to answer them when they ask you questions. Treat them as you would like to be treated and do not reveal details about this place or our meeting. Do not speak of this, any of this to any human. I repeat, keep these matters only to yourself."

He still couldn't speak. Without asking it, Ophaniel proceeded to answer his next question.

"If you break this promise, your wings will be like pasta – weak – and you will never be able to repay your debt."

He thought of another question.

"Yes, when you saved that little girl – the burning – was a part of the process. Your wings need to burn, to strengthen, to bind to you, so, you will be prepared for your next challenge."

He thought, what if I don't want to.

Ophaniel laughed and flew to the highest part of the room. Then she disappeared through the ceiling.

CHAPTER 8

NEXT THING HE KNEW, he was back in his wheelchair facing the Priest.

"Uh, Uncle Sam, we need to go. NOW."

"Oh," Sam said, as he watched his nephew wheel away. "I apologize for wasting your time, he uh, needs to go home." Sam hurried along while Hopper trailed behind him. He picked up the pace, caught up with his nephew and taking control of the handles pushed the wheelchair. Hopper ran and was soon walking beside them, albeit out of breath.

"I see, you really don't have wings then E-Z."

He glanced over his shoulder, raising a pretend glass to his lips, then rolling his eyes.

"I do not have a drink problem," Sam said defiantly.

Again, the teenager rolled his eyes, as they neared the parking lot. The priest did not follow.

Once they reached the car, Sam said, while trying to catch his breath, "What in the Sam Hell was that all about?" as he opened the door and helped his nephew in.

"Let's get out of here first." He was stalling for time because he couldn't tell him what happened. He needed to think up a convincing lie – and he was never a good liar. His mother always caught him out because his ears always went red when he lied.

"I'm waiting for an explanation," Sam said, tightening his grip on the steering wheel.

Don't Look Back, by Boston rocked out through the car speakers.

"Sorry, I had to go. I don't think Hopper could help and I didn't want him to know anything more than you already told him."

"You still haven't explained why you implied I had a drink problem."

"Oh, that. It popped into my head, and I said it without thinking. I'm sorry."

"I pride myself for not partaking in alcohol. Sure, I'll have a beer now and again. To be sociable at a work event. But I'm not like the other I.T. boozehounds. And never will be."

E-Z wasn't thinking about what Uncle Sam was saying. Instead, he was going over the information which Ophaniel had told him. He was in debt, to the angels, for saving him and he'd traded his legs for his life. The bargain by the angels, was for their own purpose – and now they expected him to pay the debt – but how?

All he knew for sure, was he had to win. Whatever tasks they threw in his path, he had to overcome. With the help of Reiki and Hadz – small as they were, he'd pay what was owed. Then, if nothing else, he'd see his parents again. He presumed that meant he would die, and they'd meet up in heaven, if there was such a place. He'd find out soon enough.

CHAPTER 9

BACK AT HOME AGAIN, the teenager went straight to his room.

"If you need my help," was all Sam managed to get out before his nephew slammed his door.

E-Z covered his face with his hands. It had been something, having his legs back again. He slammed his fists down on the armrests, as his wings came out and flew him over to the bed. "Thanks," he said to them, like they were separate and not a part of him.

"Watch it," Hadz said, who'd been resting on his pillow. The angel flew up to the light fixture and said, "Wake up, he's home."

E-Z was now comfortably reclining on his bed, eyes closed, nearly asleep.

"Tonight, you fly," the angels sang.

"Look I've had an exhausting day, as you know and all I want to do is sleep."

"You may take a five-minute nap," Reiki said.

"Then, it'll be up and at'em!"

He was nearly asleep again when Sam burst in. "Sorry to bother you, but PJ and Arden say they have been trying to get you all day. Is your battery dead?"

"Uh, no, I lost my phone," he said looking crossly at his two helpers.

"Liar, liar, pants on fire," they chided. Sam, given his lack of reaction, did not hear their high-pitched voices. E-Z shooed them away.

"That's why I always buy insurance with my plan. Don't worry, we'll get you a replacement tomorrow. It's about time you upgraded anyway. You can keep the same phone number. I'll let the guys know you'll be in touch then."

"Thanks, Uncle Sam. Goodnight."

"Night E-Z."

CHAPTER 10

IN HIS DREAM, HE was on a skiing trip with his parents. It was in fact a memory, but he was reliving it as a dream.

E-Z was six years old. He and his mother were being taught all the moves by a ski instructor. Meanwhile, his father - who wasn't a newbie like them - made his way down the snow packed hill.

They learned how to ski on the baby hill – which is how they referred to the test hills.

"Are you ready?" the instructor said, "to hit one of the big hills?"

They said they were. They thought they were. But saying and doing are two different things.

On the first try, they didn't get far before one of them fell. It was his mom, and when she wiped out, she sat on the cold snow laughing. He helped her up, and off they went again.

This time, it was E-Z who crashed, planting his face into the cold white stuff. He shook it off, was helped up by the instructor, while his mother went by spraying snow on her way. He took that as a challenge, and sped along, passing her with a smirk.

Next thing he knew, she was coming up behind him. She hit some packed powder – and left him for dust – finding her stride. Still, he dug in, giving it all he had and caught up with her. They drifted down, side-by-side, then apart, then back together again. All the while laughing like two little kids.

At the bottom of the hill, dressed from head to toe in sky blue was his father. He stood out; a sliver of blue surrounded by virgin snow – with a wheelchair in his hands.

"The snow," E-Z said, inhaling another marshmallow. It tasted even better all melted. Then he felt freezing cold and woke up surrounded by ice in the bathtub. Uncle Sam was there, sitting by his side.

"E-Z, you really scared me this time."

"What? What happened?

"I heard some noises so went in to check on you. Your window was wide open, the curtains billowing. I felt your forehead, and you were burning up. I was afraid you were going to go into a full-on seizure. Even your wings looked wilted.

"I considered calling 911, then decided against it. I mean, I couldn't take you to emergency, not with those wings. I had to get you into your wheelchair and fill the bathtub up with ice and see if I could get your temperature down. I've been going out and getting ice, asking for donations from friends in the neighbourhood. They've been extremely helpful."

"I feel better now, thanks," he said trying to stand up. He didn't get far, before he went down again.

"You have to tell me what is going on."

"I can't Uncle Sam. You must trust me."

The teenager attempted to stand up again. "Wait here," Sam said, as he exited the bathroom and returned with the wheelchair. "Here," he put the thermometer into his nephew's mouth. "If it's normal, you can get into the chair."

It was normal, so with a robe wrapped around him, E-Z was lifted from the bath and into the chair. His wings expanded, then relaxed into place and they no longer felt like they were on fire.

As he passed by the living room, he caught a glimpse of the news.

"Last night, a plane crash was diverted," the spokesperson said. "They call it a miracle landing, but here's some raw footage, taken by one of our viewers as it happened."

He watched the clip, which showed the plane landing but there was nothing else – no shot of him. He felt relieved and returned to his room.

"Be right back to help you get dressed."

He so wished he could tell his Uncle everything – but he couldn't. "Thanks," he said after he was dressed.

"I've always got your back."

"Right back at you," the teenager said. "Think I'm going to head down to my office to write a little something."

"Good idea, I have chores around the house on my to-do list I'd like to get through today." He started to leave, then turned back. "You know kiddo, you don't have to draft a novel straight away. You could keep a diary, or a journal. Write down the things you might one day forget. Like precious memories."

"I thought I'd write something and call it Tattoo Angel."

"I like that."

Once in his office, he sat for a moment thinking about the plane – wondering how he'd been able to do what was asked of him. He couldn't have accomplished it, without the help of the swan and his bird friends, or without the help of his chair. Even those two wanna-be-angels had helped in their own way by cheering him on in the background.

He focused on writing and typed in the title: Tattoo Angel.

His fingers wanted to type more, but his mind wanted to wander. He leaned back in his chair and stared at the empty screen. He needed a fantastic first sentence, like his ancestor Charles Dickens had written - 'I am born.'

When he could no longer stand the sight of the white screen sometime later, he typed -

I wish I'd never been born.

And he kept on typing.

I can't walk anymore.

I will never play professional baseball or hockey or get a sports scholarship.

I can't run.

I can't jump.

There are so many things I can't do.

That I will never do.

He stopped typing, seeing something at the top right hand of the screen which was moving downward. Flowing.

Tears. Itty bitty tears.

Joining. Growing larger and larger.

Cascading down the screen.

He thought he heard something – turned up the volume.

"WAH! WAH! WAH!" a high-pitched voice sang.

A second voice joined in.

"WAH-WAH!

WAH-WAH!

WAH-WAH!"

E-Z turned the computer off.

It had only been a rant and he felt better for it. Everyone needed a pity party now and again. It was out of his system.

He knew one thing for certain – as a writer he was no Charles Dickens.

Charles Dickens couldn't fly though.

$$*\!*\!*$$

"**W**AKE UP, IT'S TIME to go!" Reiki said, flying to the window.

Hadz was waiting at the open window. "Ready?"

So, they expected him to jump, from the third floor of his house. "I'm not going out there! Look how high up we are."

"You forget, you have wings."

"And if you fall, you'll figure it out."

At least he was still in his clothes, as they dropped him into his wheelchair. He shivered, looking down, wondering how his wings were meant to keep both him and his chair up in the air.

"What about my wheelchair?"

"Remember what Ophaniel said? Now – out you go!"

Once he was out his wings fully extended. Over his shoulders, he could see the wings in action.

The small but strong creatures lifted him up, higher and higher, leading the teenager across the night sky, while the bright starry eyes gazed down upon him. When they thought he was ready they let him go.

"I can fly," he said. "I can really fly!"

"Stop showing off," Reiki said, "and get with the program."

"I would if I knew what it was," he sniggered.

Hadz flew ahead. E-Z and Reiki lifted over the school, by the baseball field. On toward the city core. The lights on the runway near the airport were in direct competition with the stars above him.

"You are doing very well," Reiki said.

"Thank you."

The sound of an engine failing, in a jumbo jet ahead of them, attracted his attention.

"Look there, that plane is in trouble. Wish I had my phone to call for help." The engine sputtered and the plane dropped a bit then levelled out.

"You don't need a phone. Welcome to your second trial."

"You expect me to, what? Carry the plane on my back? I can't rescue a plane; I don't have enough strength. I can't do it."

"Okay then," Hadz who they'd now caught up with said.

"One thing you should know though, if you don't save them – everyone on board will perish."

"All 293 passengers. Men, women, and children."

"Plus, two dogs and one cat," Reiki added.

His head filled with screams, from the people inside the plane. How was he hearing them, through the thick metal walls? Dogs were barking and a cat meowed. A baby cried.

"Stop it, turn it off and I'll do it."

"We won't turn it off."

"But it will end, once you put the plane down safely at the airport, over there."

"We believe in you," Hadz said.

"But won't they see me? If they see me, it will be game over, I mean with Ophaniel's terms - I'll never get to see my parents."

"See you?"

"That's the least of your worries!"

"Now off you go," Hadz said. "Oh, and you might need this."

Now he had a seatbelt, to hold him in his wheelchair, as he sped across the sky toward the plummeting plane.

"We will be watching," they called.

"Will you help me, if I need you?"

"These are your trials, attributed to you and only you. We are here to cheer you on. Good luck."

"Wait a minute, aren't you going to give me any proper lessons? Show me what I need to do?"

POP.

POP.

"Thanks for nothing!" he cried.

✳✳✳

A T THE AIRPORT, IN the Air Traffic Control Tower, a Controller noticed the plane was in trouble. Unable to contact the pilot, he noticed an unidentified flying object on his radar.

Using Superman and Mighty Mouse for inspiration, E-Z raised his arms. He positioned himself under the body of the mighty metal beast and summoned all his strength.

"I thought you could use a little help," a larger than normal swan said. He nodded and birds flew in from many directions. As the jumbo jet connected with him, the real birds aligned themselves. Helping him to hold the plane steady. To stabilize it, so he and his chair could take on its full weight.

Inside things rolled around like marbles. He needed to hurry, and wished he had another set of wings, or more powerful wings. If only he were in the white room. He focused on the task at hand and prepared himself mentally for the descent. Glancing down he noticed his chair also had wings, on the footrests and on the wheels. "Thank you," he whispered to no one. Then to the birds, "I've got this now, thank you for your assistance."

Ready now, he brought the jumbo down, keeping it steady and level. He touched the front of the plane down onto the tarmac. Then, as the landing gear hadn't descended, he needed to get out of the way. He stretched his right arm out, as far as it would go and positioned his chair away from the plane's middle. He lowered the centre of the plane, then the tail. He did it! Yes! He moved away to the frightening sounds of screaming sirens approaching from all directions in the form of Firetrucks, Ambulances, and Police Cars.

Before they spotted him, he flew away. Grateful passengers inside cheered, took photos and recorded him on their phones. Soon he was back with Hadz and Reiki.

"You did very well. We are proud of you, protégé."

He smiled, until his wings felt like someone set them on fire. Next thing he knew he was burning, and it hurt so badly, that he wanted to die. He wished for death. Yearned for it. Now in a freefall, with his chair facing downwards, he kept his eyes wide open and waited for his lips to kiss the ground. Then he was carried away by the two angels, who took him home and put him to bed.

The pain did not lessen, but E-Z knew that today he would not die. He would be safe for another day. Another trial. All he had to do was survive this one.

"WHEN IS THE DIAMOND dust going to start working?" Hadz asked. "He's still in a tremendous amount of pain."

"It was a new treatment, so I can't say when – but it will kick in – eventually."

"Hope he can last that long!"

"With the help of Uncle Sam, he'll get through it. Once it kicks in, we'll see signs. Some physical changes."

E-Z continued snoring

POP.

POP.

And once again they were gone.

CHAPTER 11

A DAY LATER, E-Z had his day planned out. First, he needed to get his backpack ready for a Saturday trip to the park. He'd eat breakfast, do a little writing then head out. While he was preparing his backpack, he heard the high-pitched voices of Hadz and Reiki before he saw them.

"I can hear you," he said.

POP.

Hadz appeared first.

POP.

Then Reiki – both in their fully transformed angelic magnificence.

"Good morning," they sang in sickly sweet unison.

E-Z stuffed a notebook into his backpack and a few pens ignoring them. He hoped to find something inspirational to write about in the park. He reached down to zip up his backpack when he noticed the two angels were sitting on the zipper.

"Oh, sorry. I almost didn't see you there."

"Whew, that was close," Reiki said.

Hadz was trembling too much to utter a single word.

They flew onto his shoulders as he pointed his chair toward the closed door.

"We need to talk to you," Hadz said.

"It's...important. We did something..."

"To me?"

They hovered in front of his eyes.

"Yes. While you were asleep a few weeks ago."

"A few weeks ago! Okay, I'm listening..." In truth, he was trying not to blow his top. The thought of them doing anything to him. While he was sleeping. Without his permission. It was a terrible breach of trust. He clenched his fists. Silence. He crossed his arms. He wasn't going to make it easy for them.

Sam knocked on the door, "Breakfast E-Z, do you need any help?"

"No, I'm good. Be there in a few minutes." Silence bar the sounds outside of Sam returning to the kitchen.

"First of all," Hadz said, "we only did what we did to help you."

"With the trials. We did something to help you to achieve your goals."

"You mean you could have helped me, with the plane? I sure could have used your help. Fortunately, we pulled it off thanks to that swan and the birds."

"Uh, yes, about that, help is not permitted – not from friends nor fowl. We reported the incident in question to the proper authorities."

E-Z shook his head, he couldn't believe what he was hearing. "Don't tell me someone hurt the swan or the birds? You better not tell me that...Oh and why exactly did that swan speak to me, in English. He did you know."

"That matter is confidential," Hadz said, fluttering close to his face with hands on hips. Reiki took the same stance, and their wings touched his eyelids.

"Hey, knock it off," he said, more loudly than he'd intended to.

"Everything okay in there?" Sam asked through the closed door.

"I'm good," he said, waving his hand in front of his face flinging the creatures across the room. Reiki hit the wall and slid down. Hadz already further down attempted to catch Reiki but too late. Both angels plummeted and landed on the floor.

"Sorry," the teenager said. He moved his wheelchair closer to them. He wondered if they had stars going around in their heads like old time cartoon characters. He used to love that when it happened to Wile E. Coyote. They staggered a bit, so he put them onto the bed. When the angels recovered, he said, "Sorry again. I didn't mean to swat you. Your wings tickled my eyes."

"Yes, you did!" Reiki said.

"And we, won't forget it."

He felt bad. They were so small; he didn't realize a mere flick could send them flying like that. It was like he'd batted them out of the park, and he'd barely touched them.

"About that..." Reiki said.

Hadz chimed in, "While you were sleeping, we performed a ritual on you."

E-Z again kept his cool, but just barely. "A ritual you say?" They looked at him, guilty as sin. "If you were human, they'd throw the book at you for doing anything to me without my permission. It's assault on a minor. You'd be in prison..."

The angels trembled and held onto each other.

"We had no choice."

"We did it for your own good."

"I get that, but at this moment your apology is NOT accepted."

"Fair enough," the angels said. "For now." They chanted, "We summoned powers, the great and illusive powers above and all around you. We asked them to give you help by increasing your strength, courage, and wisdom. To put it simply, we believed you needed more and so we conjured it for you."

"I see. Apology still NOT accepted."

"We did it with the least amount of discomfort to you," Hadz said.

E-Z considered this latest information. While at the same time he was looking at his wheelchair. It did seem different now, besides the obvious colour change of the armrests.

"What's up with my chair lately?" he asked. "It's like it has a mind of its own."

The angels were trembling again.

"What did you do? Exactly? Cause I suspect you not only assaulted me, but you also assaulted my chair."

Finally, the angels explained everything about the diamond dust and the blood. About the powers which had been endowed upon himself and the chair. "As the task difficulties increase, you'll need to ramp up."

"I already know, that's why my wings have been burning. Increasing in temperature after each task. But I keep telling myself it'll all be worth it when I get to see my parents again."

"If you complete the trials in the allotted period. And follow the guidelines to a tee," Hadz said.

"Wait a minute," E-Z said thumping his arms down on the armrests. "No one said there was a deadline. Not in the White Room. Not at any time. And if there's a rule book, I'm meant to be following then hand it over, so I can read it. Also, there has been no commitment on either side. No one said how many completed trials are required to seal the deal. We need to put everything in writing? Is there such a thing as an Angel Lawyer or better still Angel Legal Aid?"

Hadz laughed. "Of course, we have Angel Lawyers, but you have to be an Angel to qualify to have one."

Reiki said, "You completed the first task without any help from anyone. You saved that little girl's life with the initiative of your chair, willpower, and luck. Those three things can only get you so far, so we got you more firepower. The most we could ask for."

"The most we could risk giving you."

"Hey, what do you mean risk? Are you saying, this ritual could harm me?"

"We did you a favour. We put ourselves at risk to help you. If you can't forgive us now, then you will one day."

"Talk about evading my question! Ever think about going into Angel politics – if there is such a thing?"

Hadz said. "The people around you may notice certain changes in your physical appearance."

"Yes, they may," Reiki said with a smirk.

"What do you mean physical changes?" he shouted.

POP.

POP.

And they were gone.

E-Z was all alone again. As he made his way toward the door, he wondered what they meant. Whatever it was, he'd find out soon enough. In the meantime, he thought about how his chair now had his blood. How the chair was an extension of himself. He made his way into the kitchen where Uncle Sam was waiting.

$$***$$

"**W**ELL, THAT DIDN'T TURN out exactly as we planned," Reiki said. "He was pretty mad at us. I don't think he'll ever trust us again."

"He needs us more than we need him."

"We could wipe his mind, like we did to the others."

"If he doesn't forgive us, there's nothing we can do about it. Wiping his mind is not an option. Without his agreement and if, not when he found out, we'd alienate him forever. And you know who wouldn't like it."

"You're right as always," Hadz said.

"Do you think anyone will notice the changes to his appearance today?"

"We noticed didn't we!"

"Maybe we should have told him, at least about his hair. it might have endeared him to us. If we explained."

"I think the changes would be better if they came from anyone other than us."

"Humans are very strange," Reiki said.

"That they are. But working with them is the only way we can be promoted as real angels."

"Lucky for us, he's pretty nice."

CHAPTER 12

E-Z STABBED HIS FORK into a plate filled with pancakes. He was starving, like he hadn't eaten in days. And thirsty. He threw back glass after glass of orange juice. He refilled his plate with pancakes, kept eating until they were all gone.

Sam laughed when he saw his nephew then continued dunking a slice of buttered toast into his coffee.

"What's so funny?" E-Z asked.

"Uh, nothing I guess."

The only sounds in the kitchen were of slurping, cutting, and chewing. Besides the clock ticking on the wall behind them.

"What?" E-Z demanded, noticing his uncle was smirking and hiding it behind his hand.

"There is something different about your, well, you know, this morning. Anything you want to tell me? Like why?"

The two creatures popped in and each sat upon one of E-Z's shoulders. They were eavesdropping and he didn't like their uninvited intrusion at all, so he swatted them away.

POP.

POP.
They disappeared.

"Not sure what you mean."

Sam poured himself another cup of coffee. "Is it for a girl? Because any girl, should accept you as you are."

E-Z laughed. "No girl. You're way off base."

Both were quiet for another few moments bar the clock ticking.

"I packed a bag and I'm going to go to the park after I do a little writing this morning. I'm taking a notepad and some pens in case the park inspires me."

"Sounds like a plan but first you help me tidy up," Sam said rising from the table.

The teenager pushed his chair back, together they cleaned up quickly. E-Z went to his office and closed the door behind him as the front doorbell sounded.

Sam let in Arden and PJ. "He's in his office working. Is he expecting you? If he is, he said nothing to me about it."

"I sent him a text, but he didn't answer," PJ said.

"So, we figured we'd pop round and take him out today. Make sure he had a little fun. That guy works too much. Mom said she'd drive us there. Just need to check with E-Z then give her a call."

"My nephew is keen on this book he's writing. He might object."

"One way or another we are taking him out of here today," PJ said.

"He was planning on going to the park, after he did a little writing. But go on down, he can meet you there later?" Sam returned to the kitchen, taking some ground beef out of the freezer. He checked the cupboard for sauce, spaghetti, eggs, onions, breadcrumbs, and spinach. He had everything needed to make spaghetti and meatballs later.

The two boys made their way along the corridor after hanging up their coats.

Sam shrugged into his coat. He had been putting off cutting the lawn for a while now. Today was the day he would tend to it.

E-Z was trying to write, but the creativity wasn't flowing. When his friends arrived – he was happy for the interruption. He opened Facebook, pretending he was checking out the updates. "Uh, hi guys." He turned his chair toward them.

"Whoa man, what the heck happened to your hair? Have you been to the beauty salon without us?"

"Did you show them a photo and ask for a reversed Pepe Le Pew look?"

"And your eyebrows too! I didn't even know they could dye those?"

E-Z ran his fingers through his hair, having zero idea what they were talking about. Wait a minute – was that what Sam had been referring to?

"And his eyes, they're different, too."

Arden bent down, "Yeah, they have gold flecks in them. Awesome!"

"Hey man, back off will you," E-Z said. "You two are freaking me out. Invading my space is not cool."

"At least he doesn't smell like Pepe," Arden said backing off. PJ joined him on the other side of the room where they whispered amongst themselves.

"Mind if we take a photo?"

E-Z smiled and said, "Mozzarella."

PJ showed the shot he'd taken to Arden. "See!" they said doing the big reveal.

E-Z couldn't believe what he was seeing. His blond hair had a black streak running down the middle, and grey flecks on the temples. Grey! He zoomed in, they were right, his eyes had golden flecks in them. His mind flashed back to the diamond dust, is that what diamond dust looked like? Those two idiot angels did this! And they better know how to fix it! Next time he saw them, he'd make them pay. In the meantime, he attempted to diffuse the situation.

"Big deal. I had a rough night."

Arden asked, "What aren't you telling us?"

PJ added, "Your hair is turning grey and you're still in high school. You think that's normal?"

"I think he's right; we are making a big deal about nothing. What did your uncle say about it?"

"He didn't notice – or if he did, he didn't say anything."

"What? You mean to tell me Sam, didn't even notice?"

"Were his eyes open?"

E-Z tried to remember. First, Uncle Sam had asked if he had something to tell him. Was that what he meant?

"Just a second," E-Z said, as he made his way to the bathroom. He used the mirror's ten times magnification to take a closer look. He gasped. The stars or flecks in his eyes were different. Not detrimental, in fact, they made him look cool. He examined the grey hairs along his temples.

So what? He'd been through a lot with his parents dying. Plus, the day-to-day pressures of high school. And getting used to the wheelchair. Not to mention dealing with the archangels and the trials.

His hair turning prematurely grey was not a problem. He moved the mirror around, running his fingers through his hair. The texture was different when he touched the black stripe. It felt coarse, bristle-like. Not a problem, he'd slap some gel onto it and...

Outside the lawnmower kicked into gear. Sam was finally doing the dreaded deed. Before the accident, mowing the lawn had been E-Z's most loathed chore.

"YEOW!" Sam cried as the lawnmower coughed to a halt.

E-Z's chair lurched toward the front door which flew open by itself. He took off, missing the steps and landing on the lawn behind Sam.

"Darn it!" Sam exclaimed. He'd hit a stone with the lawn mower, and it flew up and hit him near his eye. Droplets of blood dripped down his cheek and pooled on the grass.

The wheelchair moved to where the blood was, slurping it up with the wheels.

"Are you okay?"

"I'm fine," Sam said. He dug into his pocket, pulled out a handkerchief and held it to his wound.

Arden and PJ arrived. "We heard the scream."

"I'm okay, really," Sam said. "A little accident. No need for worry or concern. Let's go back inside."

He grabbed the handles of the wheelchair and pushed. It was extremely difficult to maneuver it on the grass.

Meanwhile Arden brought the lawn mower and stowed it away in the shed.

"Have you gained weight?" PJ asked noticing the difficulty Sam was having.

"I ate about twenty pancakes this morning."

"Maybe the black streak is heavier than your normal hair?" Arden said rejoining them with a smirk.

"Oh, they noticed," Sam said.

"Yeah, they've been razzing me about it since they arrived. Why didn't you say anything?"

Now inside, E-Z took out a band-aid and put it onto his Uncle's wound.

"It was a subtle change," Sam said. "Not!" he smiled. "Oh, and have you ever considered going into the nursing profession? You have a delicate touch."

PJ and Arden scoffed.

CHAPTER 13

E-Z AND HIS FRIENDS returned to his office. He decided to stick close to home in case Sam needed him. Sam was too busy cooking dinner to think about what could have happened with the lawnmower.

"Dinner's ready," he called a few hours later. "Come and get it."

E-Z led the way, "It smells delicious!"

They sat down and passed around the food and condiments.

"You've got quite a shiner there already," Arden said to Sam.

Sam who until now didn't know he had a visible wound and now wore it with pride. He stabbed into another meatball and put it onto his plate.

"What happened out there anyway," PJ inquired.

"It was a stone. Got caught in the mower and hit me." He continued pushing his food around on the plate. "How's the writing going?" he asked his nephew turning the attention away from himself.

"I didn't have time to get into it this morning."

Sam changed the subject and asked if anything was going on at school or on the team.

"We have a practice this evening," PJ said.

"And we're hoping E-Z will catch in tomorrow's game."

E-Z shook his head, for a definite no and continued eating.

"One inning, only one and if you don't want to continue playing, that's fine with us," Arden said.

"Great idea," Uncle Sam said. "Dip your toe in. If it doesn't feel right, get out. What do you have to lose?"

PJ opened his mouth to say something but decided not to. He jabbed a meatball into his gob. He chewed, had a drink. "When you're there, E-Z, you boost everyone's morale. The guys think a lot of you. Always have, always will."

"Ok," E-Z said. "I'll sit on the bench if you think it will help. After dinner, let's go down to the park and practice a bit. See how things go."

"Fair enough," PJ said.

They thanked Sam for a terrific dinner.

"You did the cooking, so we'll clean up," Arden offered.

E-Z and PJ exchanged glances.

When Sam was out of earshot, PJ said, "You're such a kiss up."

Arden splashed a little water in PJ's direction, but E-Z caught most of it in the face.

PJ returned a splash which splattered across the kitchen floor, hitting Sam's shoes.

"The mop and bucket are in the closet," he said, grabbing his coat on the way out.

They finished cleaning up, by then they were mostly dry, other than E-Z who changed his shirt. Finally, they arrived at the baseball diamond, and it was already occupied.

"Great," E-Z said. "Let's go."

On the sidelines, were a few girls from the opposing team's cheerleading squad. One, a red-haired girl, glanced in E-Z's direction. She did a cartwheel and landed with ease.

"Guess we could stay for a bit," E-Z said.

They made their way across the field to the benches. They had to at least say hello, otherwise they'd look like jerks.

The little red-haired girl whispered something to her friend, and they giggled.

E-Z was certain they were laughing at him.

"We've got company," the red-haired girl said.

"Yeah, a wheelchair dude with zebra hair and two nerds," the third baseman shouted. He expected everyone to laugh at his lame joke, but no one did.

"Don't mind him," the red-haired girl's friend said. "He's pathetic."

"Shove off," the left fielder shouted. "There's no room here for a cripple."

E-Z ignored all the comments. His chair though, did not. It was pushing, revving like a bull trying to break out of a pen. "Whoa!" he said, as the chair balked, like a wild horse.

Arden grabbed a hold of the chair handles, and the chair resumed its normal function.

Behind the plate, the catcher dropped a fly and fumbled a pitch. "I see you need a decent catcher," E-Z said.

The cheerleaders giggled.

"Give me five minutes behind the plate, only five. If I'm able to catch every pitch you send in my direction, then we'll do you a favour and stay."

"And if you don't?" the pitcher asked.

The catcher removed his mask. "You buy us burgers and fries."

"And shakes," the first baseman added.

"Deal," E-Z said as his chair pushed ahead.

He sat patiently while Arden buckled on his kneepads. PJ pulled the chest protector over his head and applied the catcher's mask to his face. E-Z crammed his fist into the catcher's mitt.

"Right, toss me the ball," E-Z commanded.

"I hope you know what you're doing mate," Arden and PJ said.

"Trust me" E-Z said. He wheeled himself into position behind the plate. "Batter up!"

The pitcher motioned for Arden to hit. He chose a bat and stepped up to the plate.

E-Z signaled to the pitcher to throw a high fastball. Instead, the pitcher threw a curve ball, and it was right in the zone. Arden missed the hit, but not entirely as he connected with the ball a tick and it fouled back. E-Z rose in his chair and grabbed it.

"Whoa!" the pitcher shouted. "Nice save."

"Lucky," the first baseman said.

The cheerleaders moved in closer.

Second pitch to Arden, he popped up to right field.

PJ stepped up to bat and struck out. E-Z caught all the balls easily, but the last pitch went wild, and he nearly lost it. PJ had headed down to first, but E-Z threw the ball down and he was out.

They played until it was too dark to see the ball anymore.

After the game, they decided it was a draw. They went to a diner nearby and everyone paid for their own food.

"We are going to kill you guys in tomorrow's game" Brad Whipper, the team captain bragged.

"Are you playing E-Z?" Larry Fox, the first baseman asked.

"Oh, he's definitely playing," Arden and PJ said.

"Definitely."

The red-haired girl was Sally Swoon and she whispered something to Arden, who shook his head. "Ask him yourself," he said.

"Ask me what?"

Her cheeks flushed.

"You want to know what happened, right?"

She nodded. "Did you ask your hairdresser to do it, or did they..."

"Make a mistake?" he said.

She nodded.

"I woke up this morning, and it was like this. End of story."

"Pull the other one," a player said. "Now tell us why you're in a wheelchair."

E-Z told his story. Everyone remained quiet while he did. No one ate or drank. When he finished, he was worried everyone would treat him differently, but they didn't.

They talked about the up-and-coming World Series and other sport related chit-chat.

Later when his friends walked him home, they were all quiet. He said goodnight to the guys and returned to his room. He tried to watch television, to write a little but no matter what he did he kept thinking about everything he lost. He fell back onto the bed and stared at the ceiling and eventually dropped off to sleep.

CHAPTER 14

E-Z WAS SLEEPING, DREAMING.

"Wake up E-Z! Wake up!" Reiki said, jumping up and down on his chest.

"Knock it off!" he exclaimed.

Hadz sprayed some water onto his face.

He shook it off. "You two have some explaining to do, and some fixing to do. Put my hair back the way it was. And my eyes too!"

"There's no time!" they said, as his chair rolled over, dropped him into it, then flew out the already open window.

"I'm not even dressed!" E-Z exclaimed.

Reiki and Hadz giggled and told E-Z to wish for what he wanted to wear. When he looked down again, he was wearing jeans, a belt, and a t-shirt. He looked at his feet, where his running shoes were tying up their own laces. As they soared across the sky, E-Z thanked them.

"So, you forgive us?" Hadz asked.

"Give it time," Reiki said.

E-Z nodded, as his chair rose higher and higher. Above a plane, passing the plane. Obviously not their destination. On they flew, until his wheelchair lurched to a full stop, then pointed itself downwards.

"There it is," Reiki said.

Below, a group of people were standing outside a tall office building in a cluster.

"Do you feel that?" E-Z asked, noticing the air surrounding the incident was different. It was vibrating with energy.

"Yes," Hadz said.

"Good for you in noticing this time," Reiki said.

"You mean, there were vibrations the other times?"

"Yes, but as your powers grow, you'll be able to zero in on the locations."

"And not just you, your chair can pick up on them too."

"You mean, I have a super-duper smarty pants chair? I knew it was modded, but this is awesome!"

The angels laughed.

The chair sped on while below them shots rang out. They saw people running, screaming, falling.

Toward the mayhem E-Z and his chair flew, into the oncoming spray of bullets. He flinched, as the wheelchair deflected them. He wondered what would happen if the chair missed one.

"We're pretty sure you're bullet-proofed," Reiki said without him asking. "It was part of the ritual."

"And the diamond dust should work."

"Pretty sure?" he said, hoping they were right. "If it works, then it's a good trade-off for my hair situation!"

The wannabe angels laughed.

CHAPTER 15

IS WHEELCHAIR PUSHED ON down, zeroing in on a man on the roof of the building. He'd been shooting into the crowd below, and at them as they drew closer to him. The wheelchair lurched forward, E-Z heard a strange sound, like a plane putting down its landing gear. It was coming from the wheelchair, as a metal case dropped down and landed on top of the guy. The gun flew out of his hand, across the roof before the contraption took hold. The man attempted to buck E-Z and the wheelchair off his back, but nothing worked.

A siren rang out in the distance then became louder and louder as it closed the gap.

"If I let you up," E-Z asked, "will you behave yourself?"

Although the man nodded in agreement, the wheelchair refused to budge.

E-Z needed to disable the gun and get the heck out of there before the police arrived. He wondered if anyone below was hurt. He expected ambulances were on the way. However, he and his chair could fly the seriously injured to the hospital much faster.

He stared at the gun on the other side of the roof. He concentrated, then reached out his hand. Like his hand was a magnet, the gun flew into it, and he disabled the gun by tying it into a knot. E-Z removed his belt and used it to tie the shooter's hands behind his back.

The chair lifted off and flew away like a rocket, as the doors on the rooftop flew open. The modded contraption rose, suspended in mid-air while E-Z watched a SWAT team move in on the shooter and take him into custody. The look on the officer's face who found the gun tied in the knot was priceless.

For a second or two, he hesitated considering his mandate, but there were people hurt below and he could help them faster than anyone else and that's what he did. He'd worry about the consequences later and hope they'd understand.

E-Z landed near the crowd. He gathered up the four who were the most seriously injured and as they were unconscious, he used part of his wing to keep them safely on his chair as they flew across the sky.

The chair absorbed the injured passengers' blood as it dripped from their wounds. Their blood was combined with the blood of E-Z and Sam Dickens. This amalgamation pushed the bullets out of their bodies, and their wounds began to heal.

It took several minutes for them to reach the hospital. By the time they arrived, all patients were healed, like their injuries had never happened. They threw their arms around E-Z and thanked him.

In the parking lot at the hospital each jumped off the wheelchair.

Attendants were standing by at the entrance with stretchers at the ready.

E-Z glanced in their direction. He waved, then flew off into the sky. Below him, those he'd saved returned his wave. He hoped the waiting attendants would be too annoyed they weren't needed after all.

"Thank you," a young man shouted, with a wave.

"I hope to see you again," a middle-aged woman exclaimed.

"You're a real hero!" a man who reminded him of Uncle Sam said.

"You remind me of my grandson – except for the weird streak in your hair!" an elderly woman said.

The attendants came toward the four asking, "Anyone need help?"

The young man said, "You won't believe it, but I was shot – twice a little while ago. Think I passed out. When I woke up," he pulled up the front of his shirt which was bloodstained, "the wounds were gone."

The elderly woman, whose dress was blood stained, explained how she'd been shot close to her heart.

"I'd have been a goner, if that lad in the wheelchair hadn't saved my life."

The other two patients had comparable stories to tell. They praised E-Z and thanked him again. Even though he was no longer with them.

"I think you should all still come into the hospital," the first attendant said.

The second attendant said, "Yes, you've been through a traumatic experience. You should see a doctor and get the all-clear."

All four formerly injured citizens allowed the attendants to help them inside. They attempted to get the eldest of the four onto the stretcher.

"I'm fit as a fiddle!" the older woman exclaimed.

They followed her into the hospital.

✳✳✳

"**W**E'D BETTER DO IT now," Reiki said.

"It's sad though. He did such remarkable things and now no one will remember."

They wiped the minds of everyone in the vicinity.

"He did do an amazing job."

"Yes, he was well chosen," Hadz said.

E-Z returned home, flying there as fast as he could. He knew the pain was coming, but not how bad it would be this time. He barely made it through the window and onto the bed before his shoulders were aflame causing him to pass out.

The angels returned, whispering soothing words when he cried out in his sleep. When the pain became too great, they eased it by taking it unto themselves.

"That's trial number three completed," Reiki said. "He's getting through them with ease."

"True, but we must make sure he's not identified. He can be seen, but we must wipe the memories away. I'm worried though, we may miss someone."

"If we wipe the minds of everyone in the vicinity, all should be well."

CHAPTER 16

NEXT MORNING, E-Z WAS eating cereal when Sam came into the kitchen.

"The coffee sure smells good," Sam said.

The teenager poured his uncle a mug full. "What?" he asked, with a sense of déjà vu.

"What, what?" Sam asked as he added a little cream into the cup.

"You're staring at me," E-Z said. He shook his head. Was he in Groundhog Day? The movie about a day repeating itself over and over, with Bill Murray?

"Oh, that. Is there anything you'd like to tell me?" He dropped a sugar lump into his coffee.

Ignoring his uncle, he spooned cornflakes into his mouth. "Not sure what you mean."

Sam waited for his nephew to finish eating breakfast. "I looked in on you last night and your bed was empty, and the window was open. How you got out with your chair, I don't know. In any case, if you're going out, you should tell me. I'm responsible for you and your whereabouts. Next time promise you'll let me know where you're going and when you'll be back. It's common courtesy."

"I..."

POP.

POP.

Hadz and Reiki appeared. Reiki flew over to Sam, fluttering in front of his eyes. For few seconds, Sam seemed zombified. Then he resumed sipping his coffee. Raising the glass, sipping, putting it down. Repeat.

E-Z was reminded of a bird toy – where the bird dunks its head into the glass and drinks. What was that thing called anyway?

"Dippy bird," Sam said. He looked at his watch.

What the heck? Could his uncle read his mind now?

"Who *can't* read his mind?" Hadz said with a grin.

Sam stood and with glazed eyes and robot-like motions he went to the sink, rinsed out his cup and put it into the dishwasher. Next, he grabbed his car keys and left without saying a word.

E-Z's mouth was hanging open as he processed the information then demanded, "Okay, you two. What did you do to my Uncle Sam? You had no right to...to...do whatever you did." He was so cross his face was red and his fists were clenched.

POP.

POP.

He hated that. Every time they did something wrong, they disappeared, and he had to apologize to them to get them to come back when he hadn't done anything wrong.

"Sorry," he said. "Please come back."

POP

POP.

"What's done is done," he said calmly. "Did he really read my mind?"

Reiki said, "He did, but it was an isolated incident."

"That's good. I'd never be able to get away with anything."

"We're your backup, during the trials. It's up to us to protect you and your friends including Uncle Sam."

"What did you do to him?" he asked again, as the doorbell rang. He didn't move, he waited for them to answer his question. The bell rang out again. "Just a sec," he said. "Tell me what you did to him. NOW!"

"I wiped his mind," Reiki whispered.

"You did what!"

"We had to, to protect you and your mission," Hadz added.

PJ and Arden came into the kitchen. "Door was unlocked," Arden said.

"Yeah, we told Sam yesterday we'd be picking you up this morning."

"Good morning to you too." He pushed himself out from the table.

"We need to talk mate. But we're in a hurry."

He grabbed his backpack and lunch. They went to the front door. At the top of the stairs, the chair surged forward – like it wanted to fly down. He asked his friends to help him down the ramp. Arden and PJ helped him into the backseat of the car. Arden stowed the wheelchair in the trunk.

"Hello, Mrs. Lester," E-Z said, as the three boys got into the back seat of the car.

"Good morning," she said, then she turned up the radio. The announcer was talking about a new recipe.

"Once they were on the way," PJ whispered, "What did you do last night?"

"Nothing much. Ate. Slept. The usual."

"Show him."

PJ passed his phone and hit play.

It was a YouTube video. Of him, in his wheelchair flying across the sky, carrying injured people. His chair was blood red, moving so fast like a blur on fire. His white wings were visible. And the contrast of that black stripe on his blond hair accentuated his appearance.

"Beats me," E-Z said, while scratching his head with zero sharable explanation. He waited for the angels to arrive and wipe his friends' minds – they didn't. He waited for the world to come to a full stop - it didn't. He wondered if was ever going to see his parents again? Was this a test? He flipped the phone closed and returned the phone.

"Dude," Arden said, as his mother backed into a parking spot.

"Hurry now or you'll be late," she said as she popped the trunk open.

"See you later," Arden said as his mother drove away.

The three friends made their way into school without speaking. The final warning bell was set to go off any second.

E-Z wheeled himself along the corridor, smiling to himself while at the same time worrying about who else would see the clip. Although it was amazing to see himself in action. Like a cooler Superman. A real hero. He'd rescued people. Saved lives. Him and his wheelchair were invincible. They were a dynamic duo. He wondered if they even needed the help of the two wannabe angels. It had felt good. Every single moment of it. The rescuing. The saving. The successful completion of another trial. Awesome. If only he could let his best friends in on his secret.

"E-Z Dickens!" Mrs. Klaus his teacher called out.

"Yes Ma'am," E-Z said, turning the page to read the lesson. He wondered why he was wasting time at school. He didn't need it anymore.

✳✳✳

H_{E TRIED NOT TO} nod off during class. Mrs. Klaus had her eye on him, more than usual. Every time he drifted off; she raised her voice like she'd noticed.

After the bell rang and class was over, the students parted the way to let him be the first one out the door. He glanced at a few of his classmates, to say thank you. Few made eye contact. Most looked away. They weren't used to his new status – yet.

In the corridor a crowd of fellow students and admirers were waiting. Flashes went off, as photos were taken by cameras and camera phones. He hoped the school paper was there. They'd even type an article about him. Wait a minute. He'd never see his parents again – not if everybody knew! How did this happen!? He pushed his way through. They continued applauding, growing more louder with time. A few called out, "Speech!"

PJ sidled up and asked, "Have you seen Facebook lately?"

E-Z shrugged.

"Take a look at the latest," PJ said, showing his friend the headlines.

"Local Hero in a Wheelchair." He stopped moving and clicked on the clip. It said the local hero attended Lincoln High in Hartford Connecticut. E-Z soon realized that the students thought he was the hero - he was - but they couldn't know that. They weren't meant to know any of it. They were supposed to have wiped their minds, like they did to Uncle Sam. But it didn't matter – he didn't live in Hartford Connecticut. They had it wrong. Why then were his classmates applauding?

He pushed through, they got out of the way. He went straight out into the pouring rain. E-Z wondered if he could use the newfound powers of his chair for his own personal benefit. Even though there wasn't a crisis or a trial, could he magic, or ritual himself home? He thought about this as he continued rolling along the sidewalk. His chair once helped him to save a little girl, before it even had any special powers.

He thought about magical words like bibbidi-bobbidi-boo and expelliarmus. He tried both on his wheelchair, but neither of them did anything. He glanced over his shoulder hearing footsteps coming up behind him. He expected one of his friends – instead, it was a younger student, who asked, "Where are your wings?"

E-Z laughed, "I don't have wings." On cue his wings came out and carried him off skyward. At first, he thought oh no, but he decided to go with it and waved at the kid, back on the pavement. The kid was so excited he hadn't even thought about taking out his phone to capture the moment. "Home!" he commanded. A flash of red light carried him across the sky, right on by his house because the chair had somewhere else for them to be.

They continued to fly until they were directly above a shopping centre. He could feel the air vibrating now, pulling him closer to where he was needed. The chair pointed downward, dropping him into a bank, then stopping in mid-air. Customers below continued milling about – he was out of their line of sight. He still had no idea why he was here.

Is this another trial? he asked. He waited but no answer came. If this was another trial, then the time between them was getting less and less. Where were those two angels – weren't they supposed to have his back? He thought about the other trials. Most of them occurred in the nighttime. In the dark. What if wannabe angels couldn't come out into the light, like vampires? He laughed at that weird connection and hoped it was true. Somehow, he didn't mind that it was only him and his chair this time. E-Z came back to the moment. Customers were screaming inside the mall. He flew forwards, out of the bank and into a nearby department store. The place was empty.

Touching down, the wheels turned by themselves leading him along. E-Z tried to take control. But his wheelchair also wanted control. It sped up, faster and faster. In the end, he allowed it to dominate, fearful of getting his fingers mangled.

The chair came to a full stop when splayed on the ground around 4 ft. ahead of them were customers. Most were spread eagled and face down on the floor. Some had their hands on the backs of their heads, some had their hands behind their backs.

In various positions, he spotted security cameras displaying only static. Not a good sign.

The wheelchair jerked forward again towards a young woman. She was dressed in camouflage gear with a hat pulled down over her eyes. She was fair featured, probably naturally blond, and blue eyed, the model type. She brandished a rifle in one hand and a hunting knife in the other. Her stillness wielding the weaponry troubled him. That and her excessive use of candy apple red lipstick. It was smeared, turning a creepy smile into a menacing grimace.

E-Z considered those in danger on the floor. How long had they been there? What was she waiting for? Had she demanded money? Who outside of the store, knew this hostage scene was playing out since the cameras weren't working?

One of the guys on the floor caught his eye. E-Z put his finger to his lips. The guy turned the other way, that's when he spotted a phone on the floor with a red-light pulsing. It was recording the sound. He hoped the girl didn't notice – she looked like she might lose it at any moment.

E-Z's chair took off, like a blast from a cannon and was soon upon the girl. Her gun flew in one direction and the knife in the other. The chair's metal enclosing dropped down.

"Call 911," E-Z shouted. And to the customers on the floor, "Get out of here!" They ran without looking back. Now he was all alone with the crazy girl. "Why did you do it?" he asked.

She crooned the words to a song he'd heard before, "I don't like Mondays," then grinned, rolled her eyes, and said, "Besides, it's only a game." She went back to humming the song for a few seconds, with her eyes closed. Then she opened them, and with wild eyes and laughter said, "Oh, and if you need a professional to dye your hair properly, I know someone."

"Uh, thanks," he said, running his fingers through his hair.

He remembered a song his mom sang. A true story, about a shooting. The band was named after mice, or rats.

He shook his head. The girl in front of him, resembled a character from a game he'd played a few times. Even down to the smeared lipstick. He couldn't remember which one, but he was sure she was imitating a player. "Playing a game is one thing – no one gets hurt. This is real life. If you don't like something – stop doing it! Don't hurt others."

"Buzz off," she replied, "like I had any choice in the matter."

The police crashed in, and he had to go.

They found the girl secured with her weapons tied in knots in the security aisle at a gaming console.

He headed home, waiting for the dreaded burning from his wings to hit him. He made it all the way there, so far so good. But he was so hungry, he couldn't wait to eat anything he could get his hands on.

At the ready in the fridge, was half a chicken which he ate while waiting for the cheese to melt in the pan. He downed the grilled cheese. Then made another, while he munched on an apple. When he finished the apple, he spooned ice cream from the tub. The pain never came, but he'd have a serious weight problem if he continued to eat like this.

"Uncle Sam?" he called, checking to see if he was anywhere in the house – he wasn't. He went into his office and did some homework, then played a few games. Still no sign of Sam. No SMS. No calls or voice messages. Sam always let him know when he'd be coming home late. Strange. Where was he?

CHAPTER 17

IT WAS AFTER MIDNIGHT and there was still no sign of Uncle Sam. It was the first time he'd skipped making dinner, let alone not told E-Z where he was. He knew how anxious his nephew became when things were out of his control. At times like that, the teenager's skin itched, like his blood was boiling under the surface.

Sitting in his wheelchair, he did the equivalent of pacing. Rolling his chair up the corridor and back down again. The tricky part was turning around which he did in his office. On the way back toward the kitchen, he turned on the television to create some white noise. He stopped to watch before going back to the hallway and an out of body experience took him over.

He was in the living room in his wheelchair watching himself on the television in his wheelchair. E-Z shook his head, trying to make sense of it. Why hadn't Hadz and Reiki erased their memories? Then it happened - the reporter said his name and his actual address including suburb. He got everything right this time - and he didn't stop there.

"Thirteen-year-old E-Z Dickens, wanted to be a professional baseball player. And he had the skills.

Then an accident, took his parents from him – and his legs. The orphan – turned superhero - now lives with his only relative, Samuel Dickens."

He wanted to kick in the television screen. They said it, just like that. Like all superheroes had to be orphans. Like it was a prerequisite. When his phone rang, he hoped it was Sam – it was Arden.

"Are you watching it?" he asked. "They told EVERYONE where you live!"

"I know," E-Z said. "Worse thing is Uncle Sam is AWOL. He always calls me, no matter what."

Arden had a word with his father. "Stay there, Dad and I will be right over. You can stay with us, until you and Sam figure out what to do. Leave a note for him."

"Thanks, but I'll be okay here."

"Dad says, no ifs, ands or buts. He says the reporters will be on you like white on rice – whatever that means."

"I hadn't thought of the reporters coming here. Okay, I'll get ready."

He went to his room, packed an overnight bag, then to the kitchen to write a note and put it onto the fridge. A vehicle came to a sudden stop outside, squealing its tires. A door slammed, then shots were fired as glass fragments blew out the windows. The front door blasted off its hinges, as his chair took off toward the shooter who held fire as they drew nearer.

"He's just a kid," E-Z said, taking advantage of his hesitation. He grabbed the gun, tied it into a knot and tossed it across the lawn.

The boy, who was younger than E-Z used the seconds he was tossing the gun, to tackle him to the ground.

"Not cool," E-Z said, as his chair pushed him off and dropped the metal cage onto the kid who sobbed and asked for his mommy. "Back off," E-Z said to the chair.

The kid was rolled up in a fetus position, shaking and crying. The chair retracted the cage: the boy didn't move.

E-Z now back in his wheelchair asked, "Who drove you here? And why all the shooting?"

"It's nothing personal," the kid explained. "I had to do it. A voice in my head, told me I had to do it. Or they'd kill me and my family. That's why I stole my dad's keys and learned to drive – fast."

"You've never driven before?"

"Only in games."

Games again. "Who are you referring to? What are their names?"

"I don't know. I play a few games online. A woman would come into the game, tell me she'd kill my sister. I'd switch to another game; another woman would say she'd kill my parents. In the game I was playing today a third woman told me if I didn't kill a kid who lived at this address, there'd be dire consequences." The kid took a run at E-Z but didn't get far. The chair pushed him over and lowered the boom.

"Get me out of here!" the kid demanded.

E-Z laughed; the kid had balls. "Stand down," he said to his chair and helped the kid to his feet. The kid thanked him by spitting in his face. He clenched his fists and considered ripping the kid's fricking head off, but he didn't. Instead, he hugged him. The kid started to cry again, his tears falling onto E-Z's shoulders and wings.

"Thank you, Dude," the kid said. He stepped back, put his hand over his heart and disappeared.

When the police finally arrived, E-Z was sitting in his chair at the curb. Then he wasn't. He was inside the silo again feeling claustrophobic in total darkness.

✳✳✳

PREVIOUSLY WHEN HE'D BEEN in the metal container, he was able to move around. Now he was in his wheelchair and could barely move. He tried to wiggle his toes inside his shoes – he couldn't feel them. If his legs didn't work here, then he was glad to be in his wheelchair. They were a team: like Batman and the Batmobile. In response to his thoughts the wheelchair lurched forward like a mastiff on a lead.

"Get us out of here," E-Z commanded.

He felt a sense of movement above him. A shifting of light like a cloud advancing across the sky. If only he could fly up and escape through the roof, but his wings had no room to expand.

His skin began to bubble, and he started to itch. Where was that soothing lavender spray now?

PFFT.

"Uh, thank you," he said. Even this thing could read his mind now.

His shoulders relaxed, as he formulated a list of demands:

Number one. He wanted to tell Uncle Sam everything. And he meant everything. Nothing left out.

Number two. He wanted PJ and Arden to know. Not everything, like Uncle Sam would. But enough so they understood the pressure he was under. Enough so they could support him and encourage him. He hated lying to them. He needed them to know about the trials. Why he was doing them. Like he had any choice in the matter.

Number three. He wanted them to ask for his permission, before kidnapping him. That way he'd know what to expect next. He hated being dropped into this thing.

Number four. He wanted to know where he was. Why he was always dropped into this same container. Why sometimes his legs worked and sometimes they didn't. Why sometimes his chair was with him, and sometimes it wasn't.

"Wait time is twelve minutes," a woman's voice said. "Would you like a beverage?"

"Water," he said, as the metal to the right of him spit out a shelf with a glass of water upon it. "Thanks." He tossed it back. The glass filled to the top again. He set it down for later.

More relaxed now, a song popped into his head. His dad used to love it. The wheelchair rocked back and forth, as he sung the lyrics. The chair was building up momentum – like it was trying to break free.

Seconds later he was back at home, in his bedroom with broken glass everywhere. Blue and red lights pulsated on the walls. Now at the broken window, he looked out.

"He's up there!" a reporter shouted.

✳✳✳

"Not again!" he cried, now back in the metal container. "Get me out of here!" He kicked his foot at the wall of the silo. "Ouch!" he cried. Then he smiled, happy to feel his legs again and stood up. He raised his fist in the air, "Who do you think you are bringing me here, at your every whim!"

"Wait time is now six minutes, please remain seated."

Straps came out of the walls in front of him, behind him, to either side of him. He was bound into place. He fought to break free, but the leather straps only tightened. Soon, all he could move was his head and his neck.

PFFT.

"Ah, lavender," he said. Beneath him, his wheelchair began to shake and tremble. "It'll be okay." "Are you cowards too afraid to come down here and face me?"

PFFT.

PFFT.

He dosed off.

✳✳✳

HE SLEPT SOUNDLY UNTIL the roof of the silo peeled open like the Houston Astrodome. And a thing swallowed up the light. He could feel it, before he could see it. Taking the light out of his world. Beneath him, the wheelchair trembled, as the thing above went into freefall.

It came to a full stop, like a spider at the end of its tether.

Lucifer?

Satan?

He waited, too afraid to speak.

"Hello – o – o - o," the winged creature roared, its voice bouncing off the walls.

He so wished he could cover his ears.

The thing grinned, exposing razor-like teeth while discharging a foul-smelling putrid stench.

He choked, coughed, and wished he could cover his nose too.

The beast laughed in a roar, which thundered up and down his metal prison like it was popping popcorn. He leaned in closer to the teenager's face, spewing out, "Am I not speaking your language, sir?"

E-Z did not reply. He couldn't. He was feeling very unheroic. The fact that his wheelchair was quivering beneath him didn't boost his confidence.

"DO YOU NOT UNDERSTAND ME?" the thing bellowed, shaking the metal prison to its very foundations. The thing moved closer still, "DO. YOU. NOT. HEAR. ME?"

It was like a talking cloud with a head in the centre, preparing to rain down on him with thunder and lightning. Digging his nails into the armrests, he found the courage to say, "Yes." He went over his list of demands in his head.

The beast roared and fire flew out of its mouth. Thankfully for E-Z, heat rises. Suddenly he felt very hungry, for bacon.

"I like bacon," the creature confessed.

E-Z wondered if he'd said the thing about bacon aloud. Even given his accelerated level of fear, he knew he hadn't said it. That meant one thing, everyone could read his mind! He straightened himself up and attempted to protect himself by closing his mind. His thoughts raced to foods, pancakes at Ann's Café, a thick chocolate shake, buttery syrup. Anything to keep the fear at bay and the anxiety down. This was torture, the thing could read his thoughts and imprison him forever. Was there a Superheroes Union he could join?

"Bah, ha, ha!" the thing roared with laughter.

E-Z so wished he could reach his ears, but as he couldn't he took solace that at least it had a sense of humour. "Why am I here?"

The thing did not answer immediately, so he tried to psych him out with a stare. It was especially difficult holding the eye-lock since the chair kept trying to throw him out of it. He balled his fists up, drawing blood.

The creature moved with snake-like agility, its frothy tongue jetting back and forth as it licked E-Z's fists.

"Ewww!" he shouted. "That is so gross!"

"More please!" the thing demanded, as the blood on its tongue shimmered like raindrops.

E-Z had been frightened before, now he was way beyond frightened. More like petrified – but he was a superhero. He had to gather strength from somewhere – even if the chair was useless.

"Nah, nah, nah, nah, nah," the thing sang, as it swooped nearer, then zapped further away, then nearer again. It was bouncing off the walls.

After a few moments, the creature settled in. He crossed his legs in mid-air. Then he placed his long bony finger on its cheek. It seemed like he expected to have a friendly chat.

"Hadz and Reiki have been removed from your case," the thing whispered. "Those two were imbeciles. Less than useless. I am your new mentor."

The dark creature uncrossed himself. He fluttered above, performed a half bow with a flourish and rose higher up in the container.

E-Z thought for a few seconds before he replied. Those two creatures had been loyal to him. They had helped him and looked out for him – and most importantly, they didn't drink human blood.

"C-can we discuss this?" E-Z asked. He tried to smile. He didn't know how it looked on the other side of it.

"NO!" the thing said, propelling itself nearer to the exit.

E-Z watched as it drifted upwards. Helpless. Hopeless.

"Wait!" he screamed, the thing was half in and half out of the container. "I command you to wait!" E-Z said, as the roof began to close, then the thing was in his face in a flash.

"Y-E-S?" it queried.

"I want to talk to your boss, about getting Reiki and Hadz back. They are more suitable to my, my trials. To the success of the trials."

"You don't l-like me?" the creature screeched with a voice like fingernails on a chalkboard.

"Stop! Please!"

"Bringing back those two idiots is out of the question," the thing spun like a hamster in a wheel.

"Knock it off! You're making me dizzy! Get me out of here!"

"Alright," it said, crossing its arms and blinking like the woman in the old television show I Dream of Jeannie.

The silo disappeared, while E-Z and his chair were left plummeting to the ground.

"Ahhhh!" he cried.

Then his wheelchair disappeared.

And as he continued falling, he shook his fists at the creature above him. He braced himself for the fall.

"By the way, my name is Eriel."

"Arrggghhhh!" he exclaimed.

The he was back in his wheelchair again and hanging on for dear life. They were still falling.

CHAPTER 18

C **RASH!**

Right through the roof on his house. His wheelchair tilted forward and dumped him onto the bed. Then rolled off onto the floor. They were both okay. No worse for the wear.

Above him, the hole they'd made mended itself.

"Oh, there you are!" Sam said. "Uh, welcome home."

E-Z hadn't even noticed him. He'd been sound asleep in the chair in the corner.

Sam stretched and yawned. Then he staggered across the room where a jug of water waited. He gulped down a glassful, then offered a cup to his nephew.

"What about that wicked creature Eriel!" Sam said.

E-Z nearly spit the water out.

"Who? WHAT?"

Sam continued. "That Eriel, is the foulest, most disgusting overgrown flying creature I'd never hope to meet!" He clenched his fists. "I hope you can hear me, wherever you are! I'm not afraid of you!"

E-Z's jaw nearly dropped to the floor.

Sam continued. "That thing had me inside a metal container. Now I know why you were having a bad dream. It really was like a silo. He told me I had to hand over your guardianship to him, otherwise you'd get shot."

"Oh, that," E-Z said. "I expect you saw all the broken glass. It was a kid, he tried to kill me."

"I know all about it. I watched everything from inside the silo. Did you know there was a big screen tv in there? And a good sound system too."

"What? I was just there, and Eriel said nothing to me about you or taking over guardianship." He crossed the room, looked up at the ceiling, "Is this a test Eriel? If I say anything, are you going to rescind the offer? Give me a sign."

"Who are you talking to? Eriel's not here. If he were, we'd be able to smell his stench from a mile. No, we're alone – even though I raised my fists to him. I didn't expect him to hear me."

"He probably has eyes and ears everywhere."

"They say god has eyes and ears everywhere. If he exists."

"What else did he tell you, about me?"

"He told me you were meant to die with your parents. He and his colleagues saved you – and now, you must complete a set of trials."

"That's right. I was sworn to secrecy, so I'm wondering why he disclosed this information to you."

"At first, he tried to bully me, but you got out of that jam with the kid. He dropped me back here in the house and I couldn't find you anywhere."

"Yeah, because they he had me in the container."

"He popped me in and out a few times, but I refused to give up your guardianship. After the second or third time, he said you'd requested that I be told everything and…"

"I did make up a plan to ask him that. I didn't tell him what it was – but he, like most everyone else lately can read my mind."

"What do you mean, everyone else?"

"Uh, before Eriel, there were two wannabe angels called Hadz and Reiki."

"Oh, he did mention two imbeciles. Said they were demoted to work in the diamond mines."

"Heaven has mines?"

"I doubt that thing was from heaven – if there is such a thing."

"Mind if we go into the kitchen for a snack?" E-Z asked. They made their way along the corridor, Sam put the grill on and prepared bread with cheese and butter. "While you were sleeping, I did some research on Eriel. It took a little digging to find him, but once I narrowed down the search, I hit gold." He flipped the sandwiches onto plates and carried them to the table.

"Thanks, can't wait to hear all about it. Mind if I dig right in?"

"No, go ahead." Sam watched his nephew take four bites then the sandwich was gone. He passed his own over, not feeling hungry. "I started the search keying in Eriel. Nothing came up. So, I typed in Archangels and the name Uriel was right at the top of the page."

"Think they're the same?" He took another bite.

"That's what I thought at first. Then I found a list of Archangels and the name Radueriel in Jewish Mythology. When I checked out his description, it says he could create lesser angels with a mere utterance."

"You mean like Hadz and Reiki? Wait a minute, if he created them, that's probably why he was able to send them to the mines."

"My thoughts exactly. So, I think based on that information we now know that Eriel, alias Radueriel is an archangel."

E-Z nodded.

"So, I continued digging and found this. "A prince who gazes into secret places and secret mysteries. Also, a great and holy angel of light and glory."

"Wow, he's a total badass!

"He can also create something out of nothing, manifesting it from the air."

"So, I take it from that he can change his own appearance, plus the appearances of others."

"That's right. And I wrote down some words." He pushed the piece of paper across the table. "Don't say them out loud though. If you did, you'd summon him." The words on the paper were:

Rosh-Ah-Or.A.Ra-Du,EE,El.

"Memorize the words on this piece of paper, in case you ever need to summon him to you."

"How do we know they'll work?"

"Only use them if you must. It's not worth calling him here – unless it's a last resort."

"Agreed." As he repeated them over and over in his mind, he felt comfort knowing the archangel wasn't continuously reading his mind.

"Eriel said I should help you with the trials. I'm guessing saving that little girl, was the first one you had to do?"

"So far, I've done several. The first, yes, the little girl. The second, I saved a plane from crashing."

"Wow! I'd love to know more about how you did it. I'm surprised you weren't on the news."

"I was, but you couldn't tell it was me. The third, I stopped a shooter on the roof of a building downtown. Fourth, another shooter in a mall with hostages and fifth, the kid outside trying to kill me."

Sam picked up the plates and took them to the dishwasher. "I can't tell you how proud I am of you. All this going on and I had absolutely no idea."

"I was sworn to secrecy. If I told anyone, they'd…"

"Make sure you never saw your parents again – yes, he told me. That sounds a little fishy to me. Eriel is not the sentimental type; he was like a big ball of anger waiting for a target."

"I hurt his feelings, when he thought I didn't like him."

Sam scoffed. "Imagine that thing, having feelings." He stood up. "Would you like some coffee?"

"I'd prefer cocoa." He yawned. "It's been a really long day."

"We can talk more about this in the morning, but how do you feel about the deadline? You've completed five trials, in how many days?"

"They've been random. I don't know anything about a firm deadline."

"Eriel told me that you need to complete twelve trials in thirty days. If you're already two weeks in, then they'll have to ramp it up – a lot."

"First I've ever heard that."

"He said if you don't complete them in time - you'll die."

"What?"

"Also, that everyone you've saved will perish. Sam paused, the thought of losing him now when they'd only just began. His life would be empty again, just work, home, work, home. E-Z was staring at him, waiting. "Sorry, I was just thinking about how much you mean to me kiddo. But something else he told me; he said you would die with your parents. That would mean everything we've done, all the time we've spent together would disappear. And I'm not saying I could or would ever take the place of your parents, but you know what I'm saying, right? I love you kiddo!"

"Right back at you," E-Z said. He wanted to hug Sam and Sam wanted to hug him, he could tell and yet their moved. He took a deep breath, "That's harsh. Sounds more like Eriel though."

"One more thing, he said every time you complete a trial, your soul increases. By the time you hit twelve, it'll be at optimal value. Soul currency you can use, to see and speak with your parents again."

E-Z's chair backed itself out from the table as the front door blew off the hinges and he launched off into the sky.

"Arrgghhhhh!" Sam screamed from behind him. He was clinging to the chair and his nephew's wings like a wayward kite.

"Hang on!" E-Z said. "I think Eriel is calling."

On they flew.

CHAPTER 19

"H EY, WAIT — WE'RE landing." His wheelchair began to descend.

"I wish I had a seatbelt!" Sam cried, wrapping his arms around his nephew's neck.

"Don't worry, it'll be a safe landing."

"If I don't get out of here first! Aaah!"

As they descended, E-Z noticed a circle of statues. Since he had nothing else to do, he counted them — there were a hundred statues with something in the center. Strange, he had been downtown many times, but he didn't remember this group of concrete blocks. The wheels of the chair touched the ground, but Sam was still clinging on for dear life.

"Everything's fine now," said E-Z. "You can open your eyes."

He did. "I'm going to kill Eriel the next time I see him!"

"Shh. That might happen sooner than you think." What he saw in the center of the sculptures was Eriel in human form, physically identical but not quite as large. Moreover, he was sitting in a wheelchair that hovered like a magical throne.

His hair was jet black and fell over his shoulders to his waist. His eyes were like coal, and his skin was as white as alabaster. His chin was covered with stubble, like the shadow of six o'clock in the evening, even though it was closer to noon. His lips were very red, as if he had applied fresh lipstick. His nose looked like that of a football player who had broken it more than once. He wore a white T-shirt, black jeans, and a pair of Jesus sandals on his feet. E-Z turned around in a circle, looking again at the hundred and ten men.

They were all dressed in modern clothes. Most of them wore glasses and tailored suits. Then he realized the truth: Eriel had turned 110 living, breathing men into statues.

And that wasn't all. He realized that even though they were in a business district, there were no normal sounds.

On a normal day, cars stuck in traffic would be honking and the smell of exhaust would fill the air.

The silence was disturbing, but the fresh, clean air made him breathe deeper. It calmed him down. He knew it was the calm before the storm.

He looked up at the sky. A passenger plane hovered in the air. Birds stopped flying by. In the background, clouds hung motionless. Then everything above him turned from blue to black.

The strange silence was broken.

In its place came moans and groans, as if tree roots were being pulled from the ground.

The air thickened and enveloped their throats, stealing their breath.

And below, beneath their feet, the earth began to shake. It cracked. An earthquake. Ripping. Shattering.

And the sun and the moon and the stars all shone together, but only for a second. Then they exploded and shattered into a million pieces.

"Why did you turn the people into statues? And why are you trying to destroy the world?" asked E-Z. "And why are you floating up there in a wheelchair?"

"Oh no," cried Sam, waving his fists in the air.

Eriel laughed, "It's time for you to come, apprentice. How dare you talk to me, ask me questions. I am the greatest and most powerful, but I am real, not fake like the Wizard of Oz. You only exist because I chose to save you."

"When Ophaniel spoke to me in the Angel Library, she didn't even mention you."

Eriel laughed and pointed a bony finger down at E-Z's nose. "Your case was transferred to me after those two idiots, Hadz and Reiki, failed in their mission."

"Don't touch me!" The finger retracted.

"I'm asking you again, what are you doing here, on my turf, and why are you in a wheelchair?"

"Everything will be explained," said Eriel. He lifted his legs and smiled at them. "I love these shoes, they're very comfortable."

"Those aren't shoes, they're sandals," said Sam, approaching the hover chair.

"Wait, Uncle Sam, stand behind me."

Eriel threw his head back and laughed. "'The truth is a dog that must be chained' — that's a quote from Shakespeare, which means you need to train your uncle."

"You!" Sam shouted, raising his fist in the air.

"It's hard to beat a man who never gives up" — that's a quote from Babe Ruth, one of the most famous baseball players of all time. E-Z's chair rose off the ground and flew closer to Eriel.

"Baseball is a game of balance," said Eriel. "That's a quote from the author Stephen King."

He hesitated, then smiled so widely that his cheeks nearly burst, while E-Z's chair plummeted as if it were made of lead. "Oops," said Eriel, laughing loudly.

It didn't take him long to regain control of his chair, and he rose like an elevator. He tried to control his wings, but it was too late, and he spun around like a top.

"Aaa!!!"

"Mess with someone closer to your age!" Sam yelled.

Blood dripped down his face, and Ariel returned E-Z's uncle to his seat.

"No!" E-Z yelled as he continued to spin. When he came to a complete stop, upside down, he couldn't mistake what he saw below.

Uncle Sam was now one of the statues in the circle: there stood one hundred and eleven men. He was dizzy, but a quote popped into his head, and since it was all he had, he shouted with all his might: "It ain't over till it's over!"

Pop.

Pop.

Hadz sat on the shoulders of one of the boys, and Reiki on the shoulders of another.

"That's a quote from Yogi Berra, and it's mine and Uncle Sam's!"

He now held in his hands the largest bat in the world, a replica of Babe Ruth's 54-ounce bat, and it sparkled with diamond dust.

He didn't know how heavy the bat was as he swung it toward Eriel in the wheelchair and sent it flying through the air. He sang, "Say hello to the man in the moon when you see him!"

From a distance, Eriel's voice echoed, "The trial is over!"

Hadz and Reiki applauded. So did the 110 people who had returned to their human form, including Uncle Sam.

"Of course you know he'll be back," said Hadz. "And he'll be very angry!"

"Thanks for your help!" said E-Z, as he and Sam flew home.

Reiki and Hadz erased the memories of the 110 people, then returned to work in the mines, hoping that no one had noticed that they had discovered how to escape.

Ariel continued to wander aimlessly, forming a plan for revenge.

EPILOGUE

AFTER A FEW BUSY days, E-Z finally got a good night's sleep. He dreamed about playing baseball and the next day Arden and PJ came by to take him to a game. "I'm not into playing today, but I'll come along for morale," he said.

"Sure thing," his friends replied.

Once they got E-Z onto the field, they insisted he play. They needed him to catch, and he agreed. When it came his first time to be at bat, He wanted to hit for himself. He grabbed his favourite bat and wheeled himself up to the plate. The first pitch was high, and he missed it. His pitching zone was really condensed since he was sitting down.

"Strike one," the umpire called out.

E-Z wheeled himself away from the plate. He took a couple more practice swings, then went back again. The next pitch he connected with it, and it fouled out.

"Strike two," the umpire called.

"No batter, no batter," the guys in the field chattered.

The pitcher threw a curve ball and E-Z leaned into the pitch and connected. It flew, out of the field. Over the fence. Out of the park.

"Take the bases," the umpire said. "You deserve it kid."

E-Z wheeled himself around the bases, holding back his chair from taking flight. When his chair connected with home plate, his teammates gathered around him cheering. He enjoyed it while it lasted.

Until he landed back inside the metal container again – only this time he was rolled up in a ball – and he was chair-less. Like a newborn babe, he breathed deeply as it was the only thing he could do. Wait. Babies could turn themselves over. All he had to do was concentrate, focus.

Yes, he did it. Only problem was, he wasn't any better off. He was still rolled up, in darkness. Confined in a space without light or opportunity to move hardly at all. In fact, the shape of the metal container was different this time. It was slenderer at the one end, shaped like a bullet.

Knowing this didn't help as his claustrophobia and anxiety kicked into high gear. He wondered how long he could keep breathing in this confined space. Not long. He'd run out of air in no time, and he'd die. He inhaled deeply, trying to keep the anxiety level down.

One thing was certain, there was no way Eriel could fit in this thing with him. Unless he blew the walls wide open – which might not be such a bad idea.

E-Z knocked on the walls and the ceiling. He yelled. Screamed. He remembered his phone. Could he reach it? It wasn't there. He'd put it into the sports bag to follow the no phones allowed on the field rule.

Outside of the container, there were troubling sounds. Scratching. Rats? No, not rats. He could deal with many things, but not rats. "Let's me out!" he screamed.

An engine started up. An older vehicle, like a truck. The floor beneath him began to shake and rattle as the bullet rolled forward and bounced around.

Outside the container was bouncing off the walls. Inside, he was in such a confined space there wasn't much movement. That was one advantage for being trapped in a bullet.

The vehicle hit something, and E-Z's head connected with the top of the thing. He cried out, but the sound died away. The metal container moved again, sideways. It hit something, then returned to its original position. His shoulder ached from the impact.

E-Z wondered if this was an Eriel task but decided it couldn't be. He began to conclude that he had been kidnapped and was being held captive. But why now?

"Hey!" he shouted as the metal object rolled about and landed on the flat bottom – where his bottom was. Now the weight was dispersed more evenly. He was comfortable. Or as comfortable as he could be under the circumstances. So, he remained very still until the vehicle came to a full stop and he went over end on end.

He took a deep breath, quieted himself, and said the words aloud,

"Roch-Ah-Or, A, Ra-Du, EE, El."

As he waited, he asked, "Where are you, Eriel?

Roch-Ah-Or, A, Ra-Du, EE, El?"

"You summoned me?" Eriel said. His voice was crisp and clear, but he was not visible.

"Yes, Eriel, I think I've been kidnapped. I'm in a container. Can you help me?"

"I know where you are always," Eriel said. "The question you should be asking is WILL I help you."

"I didn't know you had me under surveillance 24-7!" E-Z exclaimed, growing angrier as every moment passed. He took a few deep breaths and calmed himself down. He needed Eriel's help, and the archangel wasn't going to make it easy for him. "I can't see the driver of this thing and I can't extend my wings. And where is my chair? I'm running out of air in here. If you want me to finish those trials for you, then you better get me out of here and quickly."

"First you insult me, by questioning whether I am angel or not, then you beg me to help you. Humans are very fickle creatures indeed."

"I know. I'm sorry. Please help me."

"Have you considered," Eriel suggested. "That this IS a trial? Something which you must overcome yourself?"

"Are you telling me, this is definitely a trial?"

"I'm not saying it is. And I'm not saying it isn't," Eriel said with a snicker.

E-Z was fuming. He so missed Hadz and Reiki.

"So sad you still think about those two idiots. Now E-Z, if it were a trial, then how would you get yourself out of it?"

"First of all, they came through for me when you nearly killed the earth. Secondly, it cannot be a trial because there is no one for me to help."

Eriel laughed. "You consider yourself to be no one?" Eriel paused. "Today you are saving yourself and only yourself. Use the tools at your disposal." He hesitated then laughed again. "Think outside of the metal container." He laughter was so loud inside the metal bullet that it hurt E-Z's ears. He covered them. Then he heard Eriel no more.

E-Z closed his eyes and concentrated. He decided to ball up his fists and try to push the walls apart. No matter how hard he tried they would not budge. Plan B was to summon his chair which he did. He imagined it wasn't far away. Was it hovering above, waiting for E-Z to call it forth? He was concentrating so hard on calling his chair, that he didn't realize someone was walking outside. Footsteps on the pavement. One man, boots pounding. The man was making his way around the vehicle, to the back. A key went in. The door rolled up.

"He's been rolling around in here," the man said.

A laugh. Not Eriel's laugh. Another man's laugh.

Then a scream.

Then more screams.

Then running. Running away.

More screams.

Then movement. The container moving. Being lifted into his wheelchair.

Then going upwards, higher, and higher. Away to safety.

"Thank you," E-Z said to his chair. "Now take me home to Uncle Sam."

E-Z knew Uncle Sam would be able to get him out of the container. He'd need a giant can opener, but if there was one to be had, Uncle Sam would find it.

His wheelchair though sped off in the opposite direction.

Thank you!

Dear Readers,

Thank you for reading the first book in the E-Z Dickens Series. I hope you are keen to find out what happens next.

The next three books are available now!

Thank you once again to my beta readers, proof readers and editors. Your advice and encouragement kept me on track with this project and your input was/is always appreciated.

Thank you also to family and friends for always being there for me.

And as always, Happy Reading!

Cathy

About The Author

Cathy McGough is a Canadian author whose work spans children's literature; young adult fiction; literary fiction; psychological thrillers; poetry; short stories and non-fiction. She lives and writes in Ontario, Canada with her family.

Also available:

FICTION
YA
E-Z Dickens Superhero Book Two: The Three
E-Z Dickens Superhero Book Three: Red Room
E-Z Dickens Superhero Book Four: On Ice
A Mathematical State of Grace Complete Series
NON-FICTION
103 Fundraising Ideas For Parent Volunteers With Schools and Teams (3RD PLACE BEST REFERENCE 2016 METAMORPH PUBLISHING)
+ Children's Books